She had

She shouldn't be interested in Wade Dalton. He was too old, too smart and too upper crust for the likes of her. He probably read nonfiction and drank expensive bottled water—not generic-brand cola. Even if he wasn't all those things, what man would be interested in a woman who came with a ready-made family of four lively children?

Despite everything that had warned her to stay away from him, there was something that captured her attention. What had happened to her own vow to forget men? It had fled when she saw him playing with her nieces and nephews.

As she drew closer to where he stood, she gathered her resolve not to let his interaction with the children touch something deep inside.

But her heart did a little flip. Too old, too smart, too upper crust. She let the mantra roll through her brain.

It didn't help.

Books by Merrillee Whren

Love Inspired

The Heart's Homecoming #314
An Unexpected Blessing #352
Love Walked In #378
The Heart's Forgiveness #406
Four Little Blessings #433

MERRILLEE WHREN

is the winner of the 2003 Golden Heart Award for best inspirational romance manuscript, presented by Romance Writers of America. In 2004 she made her first sale to Steeple Hill Books. She is married to her own personal hero, her husband of thirty-plus years, and has two grown daughters. She has lived in Atlanta, Boston, Dallas and Chicago but now makes her home on one of God's most beautiful creations, an island off the east coast of Florida. When she's not writing or working for her husband's recruiting firm, she spends her free time playing tennis or walking the beach, where she does the plotting for her novels. Please visit her Web site at www.merrilleewhren.com.

Four Little Blessings
Merrillee Whren

Steeple
Hill®

Published by Steeple Hill Books™

STEEPLE HILL BOOKS

Steeple
Hill®

ISBN-13: 978-0-373-87469-9
ISBN-10:   0-373-87469-3

FOUR LITTLE BLESSINGS

Copyright © 2008 by Merrillee Whren

www.SteepleHill.com

Printed in U.S.A.

But Jesus called the children to him and said, "Let the little children come to me, and do not hinder them, for the kingdom of God belongs to such as these. I tell you the truth, anyone who will not receive the kingdom of God like a little child will never enter it."

—*Luke* 18:16–17

This book is dedicated to the ladies in my Tuesday night Bible study. They are encouragers as they lift my writing before the Lord in prayer.

I would like to thank Jeff Ledbetter for information about foresters, Susan McEwen and Bill Nolan for information on the foster care system, Wilma Allen for information on emergency room procedures and George Berninger for information on Fort Clinch. Any mistakes are mine.

I want to give special thanks to Piper and Danielle for their input on this story.

Chapter One

Shrieks of childish laughter pierced the air, and Wade Dalton frowned. So much for the peace and quiet he'd been expecting on Florida's Amelia Island. He surveyed the expanse of sand dunes swaying with sea oats. Too tired to get up from his lounge chair and check out the source of the laughter, he leaned back on the cushion and closed his eyes. The late-morning sun, warming his face, reminded him that he should be glad he was alive. After the battles of the past year, a little unplanned noise shouldn't bother him. God must have a purpose for his life.

As he took a deep breath and let the salt air fill his lungs, something hit him on the head. He opened his eyes and jumped up from the chair. A red, white and blue beach ball rolled across the gray tile patio. Adjusting his glasses, he bent over to retrieve the ball. When he straightened, three cherubic faces came into view. Eyes wide, three children were cowering behind the Indian hawthorn bushes growing next to the stucco wall that separated his patio from the town house next door.

Holding the ball under one arm, he approached the children, who wore shorts and T-shirts. They stood stair-step fashion from shortest to tallest. He expected them to run, but they remained fixed in the spot. Their eyes grew wider as he drew nearer.

He stopped on the small patch of grass at the edge of the patio and stared at the children. "Does this belong to you?"

A little girl with sun-lightened streaks in her shoulder-length dark-brown hair gazed at him with cocoa-colored eyes. Tiny freckles dotted her cheeks and nose. The tallest of the trio, she appeared to be the oldest. She pointed at the boy standing closest to the dunes. "Jack threw it."

Wade looked down at the boy. "You must be Jack."

"Yes, sir." The boy, who sported a buzz cut that made his blond hair nearly invisible, vigorously nodded his head. Hunching his shoulders, he took a step back. He pointed his finger at the middle child, a little girl with chin-length straight brown hair and eyes the color of coffee with cream. "It's her ball. It's her fault. She wouldn't share."

"What's goin' on here?" A female voice with a sugary southern accent—the same as the children's—made Wade look up.

A young woman with a toddler at her heels emerged from behind the wall. She wore a loosely fit aqua tunic that stopped just above her knees. A cascade of chestnut curls fell around her shoulders. Wade's heart nearly stopped, and his mouth went dry. All he could do was stare.

Before he could answer, the younger of the two girls spoke. "Jack threw my ball and hit that man."

The young woman scooped up the toddler in her

arms. "I'm terribly sorry the kids are bothering you, sir." She extended her free hand. "I'm Cassie Rankin."

Wade continued to stare. He couldn't put together a coherent thought. His heart was hammering, and his brain refused to work. Still no words formed on his lips. He'd never been so dumbstruck.

"Are…are you okay?" The young woman wrinkled her brow as her gray eyes studied him.

Nodding, he gathered his wits and shook her hand. He tried to laugh, but all he could manage was a sorry excuse for a chuckle. "Yeah. I'm Wade Dalton. Nice to meet you. I… You took me by surprise. And the children…"

"Well, they won't be bothering you anymore."

"Is he gonna whup us?" Jack asked, cowering behind the older girls.

Color rose in Cassie's cheeks as she glanced at the little boy. "No, Jack."

Wade wondered why the boy had asked a question like that. Did the woman abuse the children? And who was she, anyway—the babysitter, the nanny? Surely they weren't hers. She seemed much too young to have a child the age of the older girl. Still, the child did resemble her. Questions crashed through his mind like the breakers on the beach.

"Sorry about that," she put in, before Wade could say anything. Obviously still embarrassed, she peered at him through long, dark lashes. "Are you here on vacation?"

Wade shook his head, knowing he'd used a lot of vacation time during his treatments for Hodgkin's disease. "No. I'm renting the place while I'm working in the area. Are *you* on vacation?"

"No, sir, we're going to live here," the younger girl

volunteered. Then she scurried behind Cassie, as if she'd suddenly remembered that she was talking with an unfriendly stranger.

"Where is everyone?" another woman's voice called from inside Cassie's town house.

"It's Miss Angie!" the younger girl yelled and went racing across the patio, her pink flip-flops slapping against her feet as she ran.

The little girl disappeared through the sliding patio door, then quickly reappeared, followed by a middle-aged woman with frosted-brown hair and a no-nonsense tan business suit. Cassie gave the woman a hug. The thought of her giving *him* a hug suddenly flitted through his mind. Amazed at his own foolish thinking, he pushed the idea away. He had to get his head on straight. He couldn't be having crazy thoughts about the beautiful young woman next door.

The older woman reached down and ruffled the smaller girl's hair. "How're you doing?"

"Good, ma'am. It's fun here." The little girl clapped her hands. "We went to the pool this morning."

"Did you go to the beach, too?"

The little girl nodded. "But only for a little walk. We get to go back there this afternoon to play. That's why we were practicing with the ball."

Wade took a step back, wondering if he could slip away quietly. But then the child pointed at him. "Jack hit that man with the ball."

All eyes turned in Wade's direction. He tried to smile, even though he felt like a specimen under a microscope.

The newcomer extended her hand. "Hello. I'm Angie Clark. I'm a friend of Cassie's."

"Wade Dalton." He shook her hand. "Nice to meet you. I live next door."

"I'm hungry!" Jack hollered, tugging on Cassie's tunic. "I wanna eat."

Cassie looked down at the boy, then up at Angie. "I was just fixin' to call the kids for lunch when all the commotion happened."

"Wonderful." Looking at Wade, Angie gestured toward him. "Since you're going to be Cassie's neighbor, why don't you join us for lunch, and we can all get to know each other?"

What could he say? He hadn't eaten yet, but he didn't really want to eat lunch with a bunch of noisy kids. Still, he'd appear rude if he turned down the invitation. Besides, didn't he want to figure out why Cassie Rankin was in charge of these four children? Finally, he nodded. "Sure."

The younger girl poked her head out from behind Cassie. "We're having macaroni and cheese. Miss Angie likes macaroni and cheese. Do you?"

He groaned inwardly. He hated macaroni and cheese. Why had he said yes to lunch? Because his mind was completely transfixed by a sweet southern drawl, that was why. And Cassie was going to think he didn't have a brain in his head if it took him forever to answer a simple question. "I don't know. I haven't had it in a long time."

"It's ready. Let's eat." Still holding the toddler, Cassie smiled at him. The older children jostled to get inside, and Angie followed them. Cassie lingered in the doorway, her gaze still on him. "You'll have to excuse the mess. We just arrived, and we haven't finished unpacking yet."

"No problem." Trying to unscramble his senses, he followed her through the door. After his eyes adjusted to the dimmer lighting inside, he noticed several beat-up hard-sided suitcases sitting at the foot of the stairs. A cardboard box overflowing with well-used toys occupied a space near the front door.

When he entered the eating area off the kitchen, the children were already seated at the table. Cassie put the toddler in a high chair and strapped him in. Angie put plates on the table, and Cassie proceeded to dish out the macaroni and cheese. She glanced up at him and pointed at the chair at the end of the table. "You can sit there."

After Wade and Angie joined the children at the table, Jack immediately grabbed his fork and started shoveling his lunch into his mouth.

"Jack, where are your manners?" Although she spoke with a soft voice, Cassie's stern tone made the little girls jump. "What do we do before we eat?"

"Pray," the little girls chorused, then immediately folded their hands and bowed their heads.

Jack did the same, and Cassie glanced at Wade. "I hope you don't mind."

"No." Wade shook his head. "I usually pray before meals myself."

"Good. Then you can say the blessing for us."

Wade bowed his head and gave a short prayer of thanks for the food. When he looked up, Jack had resumed eating as though nothing had happened. Cassie sat at the other end of the table, and helped the youngest with his food. Wade examined his plate and noticed the pieces of hot dog mixed in with the macaroni and cheese. Tube steak. That was what his dad had jokingly called hot dogs when Wade was a kid. He took a bite. Not bad. He took another bite. Maybe that was what macaroni and cheese had needed all along—a little tube steak.

As Wade ate, he looked at the older girl. "I know your brother's name, but you never told me yours."

She gazed up at him with those big brown eyes and answered him in a voice barely above a whisper. "My name's Taylor."

"My name's Makayla, and I'm five," the other girl put in. "I get to go to kindergarten when school starts. And that's Danny." She pointed to the toddler in the high chair. "And your name's Wade. I heard you tell Aunt Cassie."

Ah. An aunt. Were they just visiting? No, they'd said they were living here. Hoping for more answers, he looked toward Cassie.

She frowned at Makayla. "You must call him Mr. Dalton."

"Yes, ma'am." Makayla eyed Wade, appearing unconvinced. "Is that what you want me to call you?"

He glanced from the little girl to her aunt. "She can call me Mr. Wade if that's okay with you."

Cassie nodded. "As long as you don't mind, sir."

"I don't." There was that "sir" again. It didn't seem strange coming from the children, but when Cassie called him sir, it made him feel old. Did he look that old? He smiled at her, even though she was making him feel ancient. Then he turned his attention to the girls. "I'm glad to meet you young ladies. How old are you, Taylor?"

Trying to hide a smile, she lowered her gaze. "Seven."

"And Jack's three, and Danny's still one, but he'll be two soon." Makayla bounced in her chair as she spouted the information. "Would you like to marry my aunt so we can have a daddy? My mom and stepdaddy are in prison. Aunt Cassie is taking care of us. She's going to be our new mom."

Wade looked across the table at Cassie. Her tan couldn't hide the pink tinge creeping across her cheeks. Would she explain, or was she too embarrassed? He wondered whether the bad stuff had anything to do with Jack's question about getting whupped. Had their parents abused them? Was that why they were in prison?

"Makayla, Mr. Dalton can't be your daddy. We've only just met him." Shaking her head, Cassie looked at Angie and grimaced. Then she glanced his way and smiled wryly. "Sorry, sir. Makayla is good at revealing the family secrets."

"Aunt Cassie, he said we should call him Mr. Wade. You should call him that, too," Makayla instructed.

Trying to temper a smile, Wade marveled at this sprite of a girl, who was quite entertaining—though probably not to her aunt. The child was definitely a handful, he could tell. He gazed at Cassie, and his pulse beat a little faster.

Every time he looked at this beautiful young woman, his insides did crazy things. How was he going to deal with that, when they were going to be here permanently—not just on vacation? He didn't have any business being interested in a woman who was at least a dozen years his junior—especially one who kept calling him sir. Besides, his health issues would probably scare her away.

Cassie sighed. "Makayla, please mind your manners. Remember, you're not in charge here."

"Yes, ma'am." The little girl hung her head. "I'm sorry."

Makayla's sudden change in demeanor surprised Wade. She obviously wanted to please her aunt.

How had these children come to live with Cassie? She was so young. And how could she afford to live in an oceanfront town house? The suitcases in the front hall didn't testify to an abundance of money. And how did Angie fit into this scenario?

So many questions were rolling through his mind. Maybe if he hung around long enough, Makayla would give him all the answers.

He couldn't believe he was even thinking about staying. Usually children made him uncomfortable. He hadn't been around kids in a long time, and he wasn't used to a lot of commotion. Four lively kids didn't make for the calm atmosphere he was accustomed to.

"Have you been here long?" Angie asked, interrupting his thoughts.

Wade shook his head. "I just moved in. I have a consulting job here."

"What do you do?"

"I'm a forester."

Makayla tapped him on the arm. "What's a… for…ster?"

"It's *forester*." He enunciated very slowly. "A forester works to make trees healthy and strong."

"I have a book on trees." Her expression brimmed with excitement. "I also got lots of seashells. You wanna see?"

"Makayla, Mr. Wade doesn't have time to look at your book or your seashells." Cassie gave the little girl a stern look. "You probably don't even know where they are."

"I do. I can get them right now." She started for the stairway.

Cassie grabbed her arm. "Not so fast, young lady. You haven't finished eating."

"But I want to show Mr. Wade my shells!" Makayla wailed.

"You can show me after you finish eating," Wade said, then wondered why. He didn't know how to talk to children, and here he was accepting an invitation to look at a little girl's shell collection. The sight of her attractive aunt must have fried his brain.

Makayla hurried to the table and began to shovel food into her mouth.

"Slow down or you'll choke. You can only show him the shells if you eat politely." Cassie returned to the table and glared at Makayla. Then she glanced at Angie. "I'm sorry about the commotion. You know how Makayla can get."

Smiling, Angie tousled Makayla's hair again. "You've got lots of enthusiasm, don't you?"

Makayla wrinkled her little brow. "What's 'thusiasm?"

Angie chuckled. "Getting excited."

"Yes, ma'am. I'm excited to show Mr. Wade—"

"Eat or you won't be showing anyone anything." Cassie frowned.

"Yes, ma'am." Makayla resumed eating.

Cassie turned to Angie. "I wasn't expecting you until tomorrow." Cassie finished feeding the baby, then plucked him out of the high chair and balanced him on one hip.

"I know, but I showed a house early this morning in Yulee, so I decided to stop by and see how you're doing."

Cassie swept her free hand in the air. "Well, as you can see, we haven't finished unpacking. The kids wanted to go to the pool and the beach, so we spent the morning just having fun."

"I got the seashells when we went for a walk." Makayla jumped up from her chair. "I'm all finished, Aunt Cassie. Can Mr. Wade look at them now?"

Sighing, Cassie looked at him. "If Mr. Wade has time."

"You have time, don't you, Mr. Wade?"

So much trust and hope shone in the little girl's eyes. How could he say no? "Sure."

"Goody, goody!" Makayla jumped up and down. "Let's go!"

Wade stood, and Makayla grabbed his hand and nearly dragged him up the stairway. Taylor and Jack followed close behind.

Cassie stared after Wade and the children as they disappeared up the stairs.

"You have an interesting neighbor," Angie said.

Cassie turned to her friend. "I guess."

"A man who prays and is nice looking, too. And the children have certainly taken to him. That's a good combination."

"I guess. For an older guy." Cassie didn't want to acknowledge, even for a moment, that he held any interest from her. He wasn't movie-star handsome, with his neatly cropped sandy brown hair and glasses framing his hazel eyes. And yet his kind spirit, demonstrated by his attention to the kids, somehow made her want to forget that the last thing she needed in her life was a man.

"He's not that old. Now, if he were my age, you might be able to call him old." Angie laughed.

"You're not old. And I didn't mean he's *old* old. But

he's probably in his early thirties. That's at least a dozen years older than me." Cassie gazed out the window, toward the beach. Was Angie suggesting Cassie should have an interest in her new neighbor? That would never work. A man like him—serious, obviously well-educated—would never give her a second look.

Besides, in her experience, men only brought trouble. Her sister Samantha had had a dozen men come and go in her life—all of them bad news. Her four children had been fathered by three of them. Jack and the baby had the same father, and that worthless bum had involved Sam in a world of drugs and murder. Because of him, she would be in prison for a long, long time.

Cassie didn't want a man like that, or like her father, who had beaten her mother. And, when he couldn't beat up on her, had turned on his children.

"Cassie, are you listening?"

She looked back at Angie. "Oh, sorry. What did you say?"

"I was just mentioning that it's good to know you'll have a permanent neighbor, rather than a parade of summer renters. The occupants of the other town houses will probably change weekly."

"I suppose you're right."

Angie glanced around the room. "Do you have everything you need?"

"I was fixin' to go to the grocery store."

"Then it's a good thing I showed up. Let me go for you. That way, you won't have to drag the kids along, and they won't have to wait to go to the beach."

"You don't have to do that."

"Oh, but I want to. I haven't been to the shops on

Centre Street in ages. I'll check them out before I go to the grocery. Do you have a list?"

Cassie pointed to the kitchen counter. "It's right there."

"Great." Angie grabbed a piece of paper from the counter. "Have fun at the beach. When I get back, I'll join you for a little while. It's been weeks since I've had a chance to just sit at the beach and let the waves rush over my feet."

As she headed for the door, Makayla scampered down the stairs. "Miss Angie, where you going?"

She stopped. "To the grocery to get you something to eat."

"I wanna go, too," Makayla begged as Taylor and Jack joined her at the bottom of the stairs.

"No, you get to stay here with your aunt."

"Do we get to go to the beach?" Jack asked.

"That's the plan," Cassie said with a nod. "You have to get your swimsuits and towels."

"We will," the children chorused, then rushed toward the garage.

As Taylor and Jack disappeared through the door leading to the garage, Makayla turned and ran back. "Mr. Wade, Mr. Wade, are you going to the beach, too? We can look for more shells."

Cassie looked up at Wade Dalton as if she were seeing him for the first time. A fluttery sensation filled her midsection. He *was* nice looking, especially when he smiled. And Makayla definitely made him smile. "Makayla, I'm sure Mr. Wade has other things to do besides go to the beach with you."

"No, he doesn't," Makayla assured in her little-miss-know-it-all voice. "He told us he doesn't work on

Saturday or Sunday. And he doesn't have any kids. He needs to come with us so he's not lonely. And he liked my shells. And he has some books on trees to show me, too."

"Makayla, go get your suit on." The little girl hurried to the garage, and Cassie steeled herself against that flutter of excitement in her stomach before she turned her gaze on Wade. It didn't work. Her stomach did another little flip-flop. "Please don't feel like you have to come. That child will talk your ear off."

Before Wade could reply, Makayla raced back into the room, waving her swimsuit above her head. "I've got my suit. I'm going upstairs to change." She stopped in her tracks and stared at Wade. "You need to change, too, Mr. Wade."

Cassie shook her head. "Makayla, you shouldn't be so bossy. Mr. Wade may not want to go to the beach with you if you boss him around."

Makayla hung her head. "I'm sorry, sir. Please come with us."

Wade hunkered down next to the little girl. "Okay. I'll change and meet you at the walkover."

Makayla raised her head and smiled. "Goody! I'll see you after I get ready!" She dashed up the stairs.

Standing, Wade chuckled. "Does she ever stop?"

"When I finally get her into bed at night," Cassie replied, her insides turning to mush over the way he related to the little girl. "And she's especially keyed up with this move."

"Well, I'd better change." He headed for the door, but then stopped. "Thanks for lunch."

"You're welcome."

Wade turned to Angie. "And it was nice to meet you."

"I'll be back after my shopping trip. Save me a spot on the beach."

Cassie watched him leave and wondered about this man who had so easily won the confidence of the kids. Their unquestioning acceptance said something very good about him. But she worried about her own reaction.

Getting involved with any man, especially the wrong man, could ruin her plan to make a family for the children. She couldn't allow them to be separated again. Keeping them together meant everything to her. She couldn't fail them.

Chapter Two

Dressed in a T-shirt and swim trunks, Wade stood at the end of the walkover. He popped the sun clips on his glasses and looked out at the beach, where foaming waves spilled onto the sand. The sea oats on the dunes bowed in the gentle breeze.

Why had he agreed to go? He wasn't a beach person. He liked looking at the water from his balcony or patio and listening to the waves as they rushed to the shore, not sitting on the beach or swimming in the ocean. He tried to convince himself that he'd accepted Makayla's invitation because he didn't want to appear unsociable. But he knew the real reason. He wanted Cassie's approval. He wanted to show her that he fit in, even though doing so might make him forget the reasons he *shouldn't* take an interest in his new neighbor.

And the kids, in spite of his earlier conflicting notions about them, had made him stop dwelling on his own problems and think beyond the walls of his neatly planned days. He'd just met them, and yet they'd already insinuated themselves into his life. He couldn't just ignore them. So he'd get through the afternoon somehow and then find a way to deal with his new neighbors.

Makayla ran out of the town house, followed by Taylor and Jack. "Mr. Wade, we're ready."

"Me, too." Wade picked up his beach chair and slung a towel over his shoulder. "But shouldn't we wait for your aunt?"

"She's coming. Let's go."

"Wait here. She needs help." He rushed to Cassie, who was carrying Danny and struggling to pull a cart that contained towels, a beach umbrella, a chair and other paraphernalia. He grabbed the cart, because he was more comfortable doing that than taking care of a toddler. Dealing with the older children was something he could handle, but one as young as Danny made him nervous.

"Thanks," Cassie said, balancing the little boy on one hip.

When they reached the end of the dunes walkover, the children scampered down the stairs. Wade carefully maneuvered the cart down each step until it rested on the sand. Pulling the cart through the soft sand was a more difficult task than he'd expected. A giant dune still lay between him and the packed sand near the water.

Cassie turned as the wheels of the cart dug into the sand, bringing the cart to a standstill. "Kids, give Mr. Dalton a hand."

Makayla put a hand on one hip. "It's Mr. *Wade,* you know."

"Okay, Makayla, please help *Mr. Wade* with the cart."

Cassie appeared to be struggling to keep a smile from curving her mouth.

With the children's help, Wade soon had the cart on the other side of the mountainous dune. "Thanks for the help."

"I'm strong. I can help lots." Jack held up one arm in an attempt to flex his unimpressive muscles.

Not to be outdone, Makayla jumped in front of Jack to show off *her* muscles. "I'm strong, too. I have better muscles than Jack."

"You're both strong." Wade forced back a smile. He might not have much peace and quiet while he lived here, but he wouldn't lack for entertainment. Maybe God was using these children to show him how to laugh again, how to enjoy life. There hadn't been much laughter during his treatment for Hodgkin's disease.

"Taylor, Makayla and Jack, come over here." Cassie opened up a portable playpen and set Danny in it. "We have some rules you must follow. I want you to listen carefully."

"Yes, ma'am," the children chorused.

"No going in the ocean unless Mr. Wade or I go with you. You can play in the sand near our chairs. And you all need some sunscreen." She drew a line in the sand. "Line up right here so I can put it on you."

Makayla raced to the line. "Me first."

While Cassie put sunscreen on the children, Wade put some on, as well. Then he set his chair near the water. He hoped to relax and read the book he'd brought with him, although he doubted he'd get much reading done.

After Cassie finished putting sunscreen on the children, she pulled brightly colored plastic pails and shovels from the cart. "Okay, kids, you can use these to play in the sand."

The children immediately grabbed them and started digging in the sand a few yards away.

"I'm going to make a sandcastle," Taylor announced.

"Me, too." Makayla said, shoveling sand into her pail.

Cassie set her chair next to Wade's. "That should keep them occupied for a few minutes."

"Only a few minutes?"

She chuckled. "If I'm lucky. Now I need to get Danny and his playpen out of the sun."

"Do you need help?"

"Yes, please. You can set up the tent."

Wade took the tent out of the cart and popped it open. In minutes they had Danny and his playpen under it. Cassie pulled the aqua tunic over her head, revealing a demure swimsuit. She reached for the tube of sunscreen and squeezed a big blob on her hand, then rubbed it on her legs, arms and face.

Sighing, she plopped onto her chair. "Thanks for helping."

"No problem," Wade said, burying his head in his book. Besides having a pretty face, she had a lovely figure, and he didn't want to stare. He'd always believed that inner beauty was much more important than outward attractiveness. But Cassie had both. He'd learned that much in the short time he'd known her.

Cassie's voice interrupted his thoughts. "That big dune behind us makes the trip to the beach more difficult."

"You can say that again." He glanced her way, then quickly refocused his attention on his book, trying to push away thoughts of helping her put sunscreen on her back. He figured maybe God had brought the children into his life to make him smile again, but what about Cassie? His initial attraction to her outward beauty had left him tongue-tied, but her inward loveliness threatened to pull him in like the riptides lurking in the ocean. He couldn't go there. It would be bad for both of them.

Wade had seen his parents' worry when he'd been diagnosed with Hodgkin's disease. Then his months of radiation and chemo treatments had only worried them more. His fiancée couldn't deal with it and broke their engagement. There was no way he could put anyone else through that torture. So he had to forget any fascination with his pretty neighbor.

Makayla rushed up, rescuing Wade from his troubling thoughts. "Aunt Cassie, let me put sunscreen on your back."

"Okay." Cassie handed Makayla the tube. After the little girl finished applying the sunscreen, she raced back to work on her sandcastle some more.

Laughing, Cassie put on a straw hat and leaned back in her chair. "I believe I have more sand than sunscreen on my back."

Wade laughed with her just as a big wave crashed onto the beach. Foaming water surged across the sand and rushed over his legs and under the chairs. Taken by surprise, he nearly dropped his book. "Where did that come from?"

"That happens every once in a while. The waves are barely lapping at your feet, and then boom—a big one hits. I have no idea why." Cassie jumped up and grabbed her chair. "We'd better move our chairs back a little."

Wade glanced behind them at the little tent. "Do we need to move Danny?"

Shaking her head, Cassie put her chair down several feet back from its previous spot. She peeked inside the tent. "He'll be okay. The tent's far enough from the water. And he's asleep."

"Sounds good to me." Wade picked up his book and tried to read, but he couldn't concentrate. His mind was on the woman sitting next to him. So he closed his eyes and drank in the sounds that surrounded him. The waves rushing to the shore served as background noise for the chatter of seagulls, mixing with the children's voices as they played.

"Isn't your book interesting?"

Sitting forward, Wade opened his eyes. "Guess not."

"I didn't mean to disturb you."

"You weren't. I was enjoying the sound of the waves." Wade sat back in his chair.

"Where are you from? You don't sound like you're originally from the south."

"Is that a problem?"

Cassie laughed. "No, just something I noticed."

"I was born in Illinois. When I was eight, we moved to Atlanta. My parents still live there. My father's a professor of earth science at Georgia Tech, and my mother teaches physiology at Emory."

"Is that why you became a forester? Scientists run in the family?"

"Maybe," he replied with a shrug. "How do you know Angie?"

"Long or short version?"

"Whichever you prefer."

Cassie removed her sunglasses when the sun disappeared behind a big puffy cloud. "When I was in high school, Angie was my mentor. She made a big difference in my life. Kept me from winding up like my sister."

Wade figured this was his opening to find out about Cassie and the children. "Makayla said something about her mother being in prison. Do you mind telling me about it?"

Cassie squinted as the sun slid out from behind the cloud. She popped her sunglasses back on and didn't say anything for a moment.

Unable to read her expression, Wade figured her silence meant his question was out of line. "Hey, it's probably none of my business."

"That's okay. I brought it up. You should know, so you can understand our situation and pray for us and my sister."

He leaned closer to her chair and spoke quietly. "So is your sister in prison for beating the kids?"

Cassie's brow wrinkled. "No. What makes you think that?"

Wade settled back in his chair again. Had he really blundered this time? "Because Jack asked whether I was going to whup them when I got hit with their ball."

"Oh, I see." She paused for a moment and glanced in the kids' direction, then back at him. "Well, my sister's husband, Jack and Danny's father, was a rather threatening man, but I don't think he ever beat them. He just wasn't very caring. If they got out of line, he locked them in their rooms. He was a drug dealer and user. When he and Sam were high, they neglected the children. And that was a lot of the time. The kids didn't get fed, and their clothes were never clean. The house was filthy." Cassie closed her eyes, as if she were trying to rid her mind of the terrible images.

"So you got the kids when your sister went to prison?"

"Not immediately." Cassie, too, lowered her voice and leaned closer. "The kids were put in foster care. The two girls were together, but the boys were in separate homes. I couldn't bear to see the children separated. Angie helped me get everything in order so I could have them."

"So you have custody?"

Cassie nodded. "Yeah. Child protective services is continuing to monitor me and the kids."

"They wouldn't still separate the kids, would they?" Wade frowned.

"I don't know what they'll do." Shrugging, Cassie shook her head. "I'm living here in Angie's town house because the place where I was living before wasn't large enough for all of us. She's helped me so much. I owe her a lot."

"The children seem pretty well-adjusted, considering what they've been through."

Cassie nodded. "For the most part. After you're around them more, you'll see some of the effects. Taylor is pretty withdrawn. Jack is sometimes belligerent, and he gulps his food like he won't get another meal."

"I did notice that today. I thought Taylor was quiet because that's her personality. And Makayla's so exuberant."

"That's her way of coping, too. She cries for attention."

Before Wade could reply, Makayla came rushing over to them. "Aunt Cassie! Mr. Wade! Come see our sandcastle!"

Just as Wade and Cassie got up from their chairs, a

loud wail sounded from inside the tent. Cassie jerked her head in that direction, then looked at Makayla. "I've got to check on Danny. Mr. Wade can look at your sand-castle, and I'll be over in a minute."

Makayla grabbed his hand. "Come on, Mr. Wade."

"Okay." He followed her and hunkered down to examine their work. "Looks good, but you know what you're missing?"

"What?" Makayla asked.

"A moat."

"What's a moat?" Makayla squinted at him.

"Do you know what a ditch is?"

"Yes, sir. Water runs in it," Taylor answered, then quickly lowered her gaze.

"You're right, Taylor." Wade smiled, hoping to draw her out of her shyness.

Makayla poked her head in front of Wade's face. "Why do you put a ditch around a castle?"

"For protection," Wade answered, seeing again the child's need to be noticed.

She frowned. "Why does it need protection?"

Wade proceeded to explain how a moat worked, and the children started digging one. He watched, not quite believing he was sitting on the sand on a Saturday afternoon, playing with three kids.

While they were busy digging, Angie arrived and placed her beach chair next to Cassie's. "Hey, kids. Nice sandcastle."

"Miss Angie, we're making a moat for our castle!" Makayla told her excitedly.

"That's great." Angie looked at Wade. "Where's Cassie?"

Wade waved a hand in the direction of the tent. "She's taking care of Danny."

"Aunt Cassie, come here," Makayla called. "Mr. Wade showed us how to make a moat."

Carrying Danny, who was awake but sleepy-eyed, Cassie joined them. "He did?"

"Yeah." Makayla jumped to her feet and ran around, pointing out all the parts of the castle. "And see the bridge we built over here?"

Cassie smiled and nodded. "Very nice."

"I want to keep the castle forever," Makayla declared.

"Makayla, sweetie, you can't keep the castle forever. The tide will come in and wash it away."

"What's the tide?" Makayla stuck out her lower lip.

Cassie motioned toward the waves. "The water from the ocean comes way up here."

"But it's way out there." Sticking her lip out even more, Makayla pointed to the waterline.

"I know, but it'll come farther and farther up the beach. I'm sorry, kids, but that's the way it happens." Cassie laid her hand on the little girl's shoulder. "By tomorrow morning, your castle will be gone."

"I hate it here!" Makayla jerked away from Cassie and sprinted down the beach.

"Makayla, come back here!" Cassie shouted. Danny began to cry.

"Give Danny to me." Angie reached for the toddler. "You go after Makayla."

Wade watched Cassie race down the beach. When she reached Makayla's side, she gathered the child into her arms, and after a moment or two, they strolled toward the water's edge. Wade wondered what Cassie was say-ing to calm the child, and marveled at her composure.

"Cassie's fabulous with the kids. She loves them so much. Love and care is what they need."

Wade turned in Angie's direction. "I can see that. She's taken on a lot of responsibility."

"That's for sure." Angie eyed him. "I'm sure you gathered from Makayla's comments during lunch that these kids have been through a tough time."

"Yeah, Cassie explained even more to me."

"That's good. Then you understand the situation. I hope you can give her a hand occasionally. She needs a good friend. I hope that's not asking too much."

"No. It's not." What else could he say? A Christian helped people in need, and Cassie was in need. Maybe God was giving him an opportunity to help someone else. After all, he'd had many people helping him and praying for him while he battled Hodgkin's disease.

But how could he keep the right perspective, when just looking at Cassie made his pulse race? Then there was the matter of the children. As the youngest of three brothers, and a bachelor, he'd never had to deal with lit-tle children. The truth was, he didn't know much about them. *Could* he help? Was he up to the challenge?

Cassie hadn't even glanced at Wade before she ran down the beach in pursuit of Makayla. Now she won-dered what he was thinking of her. That she had no con-trol over these children probably. But it didn't matter what he thought. This wasn't his problem. It was hers. And sometimes she wondered whether she had what it took to take care of her nieces and nephews. But she couldn't let negative thinking rule. She had to be strong for them. They needed her. No one cared whether they stayed together except her and Angie.

Cassie thought about the social worker, who would come to visit to make sure she could provide a good home for the children. Cassie's stomach churned at the thought of the home inspection. Everything had to be perfect. What if Makayla acted out while the social worker was there? What if Jack decided to punch someone, as he did from time to time? What if? What if? What if?

Makayla gripped Cassie's hand as the waves washed over their feet. The little girl's tears were gone, but every few seconds she sniffled. Her tears hadn't been about the sandcastle. They'd been about the past—her life of neglect, want and fear. Could they rise above it? They had to. Cassie vowed to be strong for all of them.

But Cassie wanted to reassure her as much as she could. "It's okay, sweetheart. We'll build a new sand-castle tomorrow."

Makayla looked up. "But it'll get washed away, too."

"Yes, but we can make it bigger and better than the time before. We can make a new one every time we come to the beach."

"Do you think Mr. Wade will help us?" The child rubbed a hand across her face, leaving a sandy smear on one cheek.

Cassie gently wiped it away with her thumb. "Let's go ask him."

"Okay." Makayla turned and pulled Cassie down the beach. The prospect of talking to Mr. Wade seemed to make the little girl put the demise of the sandcastle out of her mind. He definitely had a way with this child.

The thought of talking with Wade had Cassie in a dither. What was there about the man that gained the little girl's confidence but made Cassie hesitate? The answer was simple. Cassie had a hard time trusting men, even men as seemingly nice as Wade Dalton.

As Cassie and Makayla retraced their steps along the beach, Wade sat with the other children and watched them play in the sand. Cassie tried to tell herself that she should hold no interest in Wade Dalton. He was too old, too smart, too upper-crust for the likes of her.

She had to be realistic. Even if he wasn't all those things, what man would be interested in a woman who came with a ready-made family of four lively children? But despite her misgivings that warned her away from him, there was something about the man that captured her attention. She didn't want to admit his connection to the kids warmed her heart and worked to melt away some of her resistance and distrust. But it would take a lot more than that to completely eradicate her uncertainties about men. She had to remember that she didn't need a man. *Men were trouble. Repeat. Men were trouble.*

When Cassie and Makayla were just a few yards away, Wade looked in their direction. Even though the sun clips on his glasses hid his hazel eyes, she remembered the warmth she'd seen in them earlier, when he looked at her. She tried not to read anything into that warmth.

Suddenly Makayla let go of Cassie's hand. She ran ahead, leaving tiny footprints in the wet sand. Waving a hand over her head, Makayla yelled, "Mr. Wade! Mr. Wade! Will you help me build a sandcastle tomorrow?"

As the little girl raced toward Wade, Cassie had a sudden, insane impulse to do the same thing. She deliberately slowed her pace. She wasn't some child, eager to gain his attention.

Makayla abruptly stopped in front of him.

He shook his head. "I don't know. I'm going to church in the morning. Maybe in the afternoon."

"Will you take me to church?" Makayla asked. "I've never been to church."

"We'll have to see what your aunt says." Wade stood, and his gaze met Cassie's. "Makayla says she'd like to attend church in the morning. Would you like to go?"

Her heart did a little flip-flop. *Too old. Too smart. Too upper-crust.* She let the refrain roll through her brain. It didn't help.

"That's a wonderful idea," Angie interjected. "It'll give you a good start here, and an opportunity to meet some good people."

Cassie wanted to agree, but the prospect of dealing with four live-wire kids during a church service made her uneasy. "Is it a real formal church? I'm not sure the kids are ready for something like that."

Wade shrugged. "I'm not sure. Since I just moved here, I haven't been. But the church was recommended by John and Glenda Tatum, the folks who own the town house I'm renting."

"Oh, I've been to church with the Tatums." Angie patted Cassie on the arm. "I've known them since they first started vacationing here on Amelia Island. The congregation is very friendly. You'll have no problem." Angie glanced at Wade. "The last time I talked with Glenda, she mentioned they were renting their town house this summer. She said you were a great guy and that I should meet you."

"She did?" Wade chuckled. "Then she didn't tell you I broke her daughter's heart when I went away to college."

Angie laughed. "So *you're* the guy Megan cried over."

"Guess so." Wade smiled wryly. "But it all worked out in the end. Megan's happily married with two kids now."

"No happily-ever-after for you?"

"That remains to be seen." He turned to Cassie. "Well, what do you say, Cassie? Would you and the kids like to go to church with me?"

At Wade's question, Cassie's insides skittered like the little sanderlings racing across the beach, their little bird legs moving at a seemingly impossible speed. This wasn't about her, and she had to remember that. She shouldn't read anything into his invitation. This was about God, and four little children who didn't have a clue about church. Cassie's sister had never darkened a church door, not even to get married. She'd had no use for religion or anything associated with God.

Cassie had read from a Bible storybook to the kids since they'd come to live with her, but they didn't know much beyond that. She'd talked to them about praying before meals, but they'd never been to church. Did she dare accept Wade's invitation?

Chapter Three

Heat rose from the blacktop parking lot as the mid-morning sun played peekaboo behind the puffy white clouds in the crystal blue sky. Cassie struggled toward the church, as she carried Danny and a quilted green-and-white diaper bag filled with her Bible and some kid stuff that she hoped would keep them out of trouble during the worship service. As soon as they emerged from Wade's SUV, Makayla and Taylor rushed to hold his hands. The scene evoked feelings for Wade that threatened to burrow into Cassie's heart.

Trying to focus her thoughts on something else, Cassie wished the girls had pretty dresses to wear, instead of their well-worn shorts and T-shirts. Their lack of "church clothes" had been one reason she hesitated to take them. What would people think? Her own skirt and blouse weren't exactly stylish, either, and in spite of herself, she wondered what Wade thought of the way she was dressed.

Then her stomach began to churn at the thought of

all the things that could go wrong this morning. Would the children sit still? Would they be quiet? Had her little talk about how to behave in church sunk into their childish minds? Jack, who had the job of carrying Wade's Bible, ran a zigzag path just behind Wade and the girls. The little boy's actions didn't inspire her confidence.

A balding man with a big grin greeted Wade and the girls. Even Taylor smiled shyly at the man's greeting. Makayla pumped his hand with her usual enthusiasm.

When Cassie joined the group, the jovial man shook her hand. "You and your husband have a lovely family."

"Oh, we're not married," Cassie blurted. "I—I mean we're just neighbors."

The man didn't quit smiling, but his face turned a little pink as he held the door open for them. "Sorry. It's just that you all look so much like a family."

"No problem," Wade replied, glancing at Cassie with a smile.

Cassie smiled back at him, but her stomach roiled as they entered the building. How was she going to handle this whole thing? At least Wade didn't seem embarrassed. And thankfully Makayla hadn't decided to tell the man that she wanted Wade to be her daddy.

A woman greeted them in the foyer and explained the children's programs available, including a nursery. As they went into the auditorium, Cassie surveyed the pews filled with families. For just a moment, she couldn't help thinking about what the man at the front door had said. That they looked like a family—like all the families gathered in here for worship.

To be a family….

But Cassie couldn't even think about such things. She needed to concentrate on keeping these children together—with her—not hope for the impossible.

She glanced at Wade, who still held the girls' hands. "Should we sit near the back?"

"Do you want to put Danny in the nursery?" Wade asked.

Cassie gazed at the toddler in her arms, then looked back at Wade and shrugged. "The kids have been left with strangers so much in recent weeks that I'm not sure that would be a good idea. If I have problems with him, I'll take him later."

"Good idea." Wade ushered Taylor and Makayla into a pew. Jack scampered in behind Wade and climbed onto the seat. Settling beside Wade, Jack placed the Bible he'd been carrying squarely on his lap and folded his little hands on top of it. His little legs stuck straight out, with his dingy tennis shoes barely hanging over the seat. The sight caused a tightness in Cassie's chest.

Danny seemed satisfied to sit on her lap and thumb through a battered storybook she'd brought out of the bag. Everything seemed to be going well so far. But would it last?

Moments after they settled in the pew, a man started leading a song, the words appearing on a screen at the front of the auditorium. Cassie wasn't familiar with it, but Wade sang without hesitation. Taylor, who could read, appeared to mouth the words, but Makayla began to fidget. Cassie tried to sing while keeping an eye on Makayla.

The congregation stood for the next hymn—this time

a lively tune that Cassie knew. Voices rose in harmony all around her. She joined in the chorus, finally having the sense of worship.

The song ended, and a little voice carried across the quiet pews. "I liked that song."

A collective chuckle rolled through the congregation. When she realized the voice was Makayla's, Cassie wanted to hide under the pew. She leaned over and lightly touched the little girl's shoulder. She glanced up, and Cassie shook her head and tapped her index finger against her lips.

Makayla's eyes grew wide and pooled with tears, and she hung her head. Cassie wanted to gather the child into her arms. Before she could put Danny on the pew, Wade reached down and plucked Makayla off the floor. She wrapped her arms around his neck and buried her face in his chest. Patting her back, he whispered something Cassie couldn't hear.

As the next praise hymn started, Makayla nodded her head and gave him a big hug. He set her on the floor while she wiped the tears from her eyes and cheeks with the back of her hand. His smile had Cassie thinking about having her own arms around his neck. She shook the thought away, determined not to let her mind wander into territory better left unexplored.

Makayla touched her arm and Cassie's heart twisted when their eyes met. Cassie read the wish to please in Makayla's eyes. The child tried so hard. Sometimes too hard.

Cassie understood that feeling. She'd always put her best effort into school, but it had always been a struggle. She'd nearly been ready to drop out when Angie came into her life. Angie had given Cassie the courage to continue despite the difficulties.

Now Cassie faced another challenge. Was she up to the task? She didn't want to crush Makayla's enthusiasm for life, but at the same time, the child needed to learn appropriate behavior. A fine line to walk. Would Cassie miss the mark again when dealing with the children? No. She couldn't let that happen.

Holding Danny tightly, Cassie suddenly realized that everyone was starting to sit. Her mind had wandered through most of the song service. She'd been so worried about the children's behavior that she'd forgotten to worship. *Lord, forgive me for concentrating on my troubles and forgetting You. Help me with the challenges before me. Please give me wisdom to deal with the kids. Most of all, help me to teach them about You.*

That was what had been missing all along. She'd forgotten to rely on God. She'd been trying to do it on her own. How many times had Angie reminded Cassie to put her troubles in God's hands? God, who had put the sun, moon and stars in the sky and created life on earth, could surely guide her. She just had to keep that in mind when things looked bleak.

Wade gave each of the three older children a dollar bill to put in the offering plate. Taylor and Makayla obediently dropped their money into the plate as it passed, but Jack didn't want to give up his dollar. He clutched it in his little fist, and Cassie didn't know how to make him let go without causing a scene. Hoping for help, she glanced at Wade.

Wade shrugged his shoulders and whispered, "Just let him keep it. We can talk to him later."

Cassie dropped her offering into the plate then gave it back to the usher.

"Jack didn't give his money." At least this time Makayla's whisper didn't carry across the whole auditorium.

Cassie leaned over and cupped her hand around Makayla's ear. "You're right, but he should've. I'm proud of you and Taylor for giving your money."

Seemingly placated for the moment, Makayla pressed her little back against the pew and folded her arms. Cassie wondered what would go wrong next. She wished she'd taken the time to explain what would occur during the worship service, not just tell them to sit still and be quiet.

Just before the sermon, the song leader announced the location of the children's classes. Wade leaned closer and whispered, "Would you like me to take them?"

Relief washing over her, she nodded gratefully.

Wade ushered the kids out of the pew, and Cassie prayed that they'd behave in their classes. As the congregation sang an upbeat hymn, Danny fell asleep in her arms, and she laid him on the pew. Peace at last. Maybe she could even get something out of the sermon.

But when Wade slipped back into the pew, she didn't think about the sermon. She thought about the man sitting next to her. She'd never met such a good man. How was she going to cast aside her attraction to him, when he kept being wonderful—not to mention the fact that he was living next door?

When the church service ended, several people came up and introduced themselves. The friendliness of the congregation warmed Cassie's heart. No one mentioned the kids' less-than-stellar behavior. While she shook more hands, Taylor, Makayla and Jack hurried into the auditorium, waving papers above their heads, then came to a screeching halt in front of Cassie.

Jack shoved a paper at her. "See what I got?"

"Tell me about it."

"See mine?" Makayla elbowed her way in front of Jack and pushed her paper under Cassie's nose.

Wade joined them, and Cassie marveled at his patience. Hunkered down in front of them, he listened as though he really cared about what they were saying. They had his complete attention. So often she'd seen adults listen to kids with one ear. Not Wade. His focus was completely on the kids.

He stood after the children finished showing him their papers. He smiled at Cassie. "Who's ready for lunch?"

"Me! Me!" Grabbing Wade's hand, Makayla jumped up and down.

Taylor and Jack joined in the chorus. Even Danny clapped his hands.

"Okay, let's head to the car." Wade gestured toward the door and then turned to Cassie. "We've been invited to join some of the church folks at a restaurant at the corner of Fourteenth and Sadler."

Cassie's heart plummeted. She couldn't afford even a reasonably priced restaurant. Would he understand? "I don't know. The kids were so bad in church. I don't want to have to deal with them in a restaurant."

Shaking his head, Wade smiled. "They weren't that bad."

"You're just being nice."

"They did fine, considering it was their first time. You're being too hard on them."

"You're serious?"

"Yeah. They were much better than you think." Nodding, he chuckled.

"What's so funny?"

"I just remembered this story my mother tells about me when I was Jack's age. My parents were sitting in the back pew. During a prayer, while they weren't looking, I crawled under all the pews to the very front. Then I stood up, looked around and yelled, 'Where's my mommy?'" Wade laughed.

Cassie joined in the laughter. "What did your mother do?"

"She was mortified. She had to go all the way to the front and get me." He chuckled again. "So you see, your kids weren't so bad. They'll do fine at the restaurant."

Now how was she going to get out of going? If she mentioned the cost, he'd probably feel obligated to pay. She didn't want to feel like a charity case any more than she already did. Angie helped her all the time. Someday Cassie wanted to fend for herself—not have to rely on someone else all the time. She would have to leave it in God's hands—like the children's Bible story of Jesus feeding the crowd. Somehow God would provide. The bright spot in the whole scenario was having Wade call the children "your kids."

"That was a good pizza." Makayla skipped along beside Wade as they walked away from the restaurant. "Mr. Wade, can we go to church with you again?"

"That's up to your aunt." Wade glanced at Cassie, who was carrying Danny. She still had the same rigid set to her shoulders that he'd seen most of the morning.

Makayla rushed over to Cassie and patted her on the arm. "Do we get to go again?"

With a halfhearted smile, Cassie glanced down at her niece. "Probably."

"Yay!" Makayla hurried to open the door to Wade's SUV, then scrambled into the backseat.

Without saying a word, Taylor joined Makayla, while Cassie put Danny into the car seat and buckled him in. Wade lifted Jack and buckled him into the car seat next to Danny. After everyone was settled, Wade drove back to the town houses. For a few minutes, everyone was quiet—even Makayla—but the silence was short-lived.

"Aunt Cassie, you never talked to Jack about the money." Makayla's high-pitched little voice carried from the back.

Wade stopped at an intersection. Raising his eyebrows, he looked over at Cassie. She bit back a smile and shook her head. He wondered how she intended to handle this little problem. His admiration for this young woman had grown immensely this morning, as he'd watched her handle the children in church and again at the restaurant. Her patience amazed him.

Cassie turned toward the backseat. "Makayla, we'll talk about it when we get home. Okay?"

"Okay, ma'am." Makayla said, seemingly satisfied for the moment.

When they arrived at the town houses, Makayla jumped out of the SUV as soon as Cassie opened the door. "Let's hurry so we can go to the beach."

Jack unstrapped himself from the car seat and joined his sister as they raced to the front door.

Taylor hung back with Cassie, who was getting Danny. "Aunt Cassie,.do you need some help?"

Surprise and appreciation combined in the look Cassie gave the little girl. "Yes, please, you can get the diaper bag."

"Okay." Taylor plucked the bag from the floor in the front seat.

Wade grabbed his Bible and closed the door. Hesitating, he wondered whether he should accompany Cassie to her town house or just head to his own. Her posture remained rigid as she set Danny on the walk at her front door. Wade had the crazy urge to massage her shoulders and take away her tension. But he'd already involved himself in this situation way more than he'd ever intended. He had to get away for a few moments, or he would act on the ridiculous thought.

"Cassie, I'm headed to my place—"

Makayla turned and raced back to Wade and pulled on his arm before he could finish his sentence. "Mr. Wade, aren't you going to the beach? You promised to help us build a sandcastle."

Wade couldn't help smiling as Makayla grabbed his hand. He looked down at her, and a strange pressure settled in his chest as he saw the trust in her eyes. "Yes, I'm going to the beach with you, but I have to put on my swim trunks. And you have to put on your swimsuit."

"Yes, sir." Makayla scampered away to catch Cassie. Before Makayla went inside, she turned and waved.

He waved back, and the pressure returned. "I'll see you in a few minutes."

While Wade dressed for the beach, he marveled at the

turn his life had taken since he'd moved here just days ago. He'd come for solitude and the opportunity to start a new chapter in his life. He'd figured the folks renting the nearby town houses for a week's vacation would come and go without bothering him. Even during the height of the tourist season, this little island and its beaches remained relatively uncrowded. Instead of the peace he'd imagined, he'd been confronted with four little noisemakers and their beautiful aunt.

After pulling a T-shirt over his head, Wade grabbed a beach towel and shoved his feet into a pair of faded navy-blue boat shoes. He locked his town house and headed next door. As he approached, he could see through the patio door. Singing at the top of her lungs, Makayla ran back and forth between the living room and kitchen with a towel tied around her neck to make a superhero's cape. Taylor was entertaining Danny, who sat in his high chair. Cassie, dressed in the aqua tunic she'd worn when they met, was stuffing a bag with beach supplies. Jack was jumping up and down and wailing about wanting something to drink. He grabbed the bottle of apple juice on the counter.

The chaotic scene seemed to unfold in slow motion. The bottle slipped out of Jack's hand and thudded on the floor. Juice splashed everywhere. Before Makayla could stop, she slid on the wet floor and landed on her behind. She began to cry.

Cassie slapped the beach bag on the table and glared at Jack. One loud curse word echoed through the room and punctuated her glare. Obviously, her patience, which he'd admired earlier, had just run out.

Surprised by her profanity, he stood there gaping. When

he finally gained his senses, he started to back away. But before he could get out of sight, Cassie looked up.

Her eyes grew wide as her cheeks flamed with red. She covered her mouth with both hands, and her shoulders sagged. Immediately looking away, she helped Makayla to her feet. Then she grabbed some paper towels and began mopping up the mess on the floor.

Wade stepped into the kitchen. "Let me help."

Cassie glanced at him. Misery painted every inch of her pretty face. Tears welling in her eyes, she shook her head. "Please…just go away."

He stepped closer. "I'm going to help."

Without another word, she turned and continued mopping.

Lifting Danny from the high chair, Wade looked at the three older children, who stood in bewildered silence. "Come with me, kids."

Amazed that he was actually taking care of a baby, Wade led them upstairs to one of the bedrooms. When they were all in the room, Wade set Danny on the bed covered in a pink-and-green floral-print coverlet with lacy trim. He looked at Taylor. "Would you watch Danny?"

"Yes, sir." Taylor joined the little boy on the bed and began playing patty-cake with him. He laughed, seemingly oblivious of the tensions of the past few minutes.

Wade turned to the other two children. "Makayla and Jack, I want you to sit on the other bed."

Nodding, they scrambled to obey. They sat on the bed and, wide-eyed, stared at him without saying a word.

"I want you to sit here and behave until I come back. Can you do that?"

They nodded, still staring. Even Makayla was silent, her hands folded in her lap and her little legs dangling over the edge of the bed.

"Good. Now I'm going to help your aunt clean up the mess."

When Wade returned to the kitchen, Cassie was still on her hands and knees, wiping a big yellow sponge across the off-white tile floor. She sat back on her haunches and ran a hand across her face to wipe away her tears. She sniffled and started wiping the floor again.

He ached to gather her into his arms and comfort her. But if he tried to soothe her, his actions might not be just brotherly. Every time he looked at her, he thought about their connection as a man and a woman. Could he hold her without letting those thoughts take over?

Stepping closer, he whispered, "Cassie."

She looked up, then quickly returned her gaze to the floor and scrubbed madly at non-existent dirt on the tile. "I'm so embarrassed. You must think I'm awful."

He hunkered down beside her. "I don't think you're awful. I think you've got a lot of love for your nieces and nephews."

Eyes filled with tears, she looked at him again. "If you love someone, you shouldn't swear at them."

Putting a hand on her arm, Wade nodded. "That's true, but sometimes we all do things we wish we hadn't done."

"I try so hard to be a good Christian, but sometimes the old ways just come crashing back." She sank to the floor and let the sponge fall from her hand. Sighing heavily, she covered her face with her hands. "I'm so bad." Her words came out in strangled tones. "How can I take care of these kids? Will I ever get it right?"

Wade sat down next to her on the floor and put an arm around her shoulders. He couldn't let himself have anything other than brotherly feelings for this young woman. *Think of her as a sister. That's right. A sister.* After all, she was his sister in Christ, and she needed his help.

He gave her shoulders a squeeze. "You'll do fine. If you ever need something, just let me know. I want to help."

"I don't know how you can help me break a lifelong habit of cursing."

Her dejected tone touched him. "We could pray about it."

"God's going to listen to my prayers, after the way I talked?"

"Yes, God wants us to ask for forgiveness."

Cassie looked at him as a little smile curved her lips. "Thank you for reminding me I'll be forgiven if I ask. Will you pray with me?"

Nodding, Wade bowed his head as Cassie poured her heart out to God. When she'd finished praying, she looked at him again with that little smile. He had to think of something other than the way she made his pulse race. "Are you feeling better now?"

"Yes, sir." She jumped to her feet. "Now, I need to talk to the kids and tell them I'm sorry."

"Okay, let's go." He followed her up the stairs.

Wade leaned against the doorjamb while Cassie sat on the bed with Danny and Taylor and summoned Jack and Makayla to join her. With those now-familiar wide-eyed expressions, the kids huddled around her.

"Kids, Aunt Cassie is so sorry she yelled. I shouldn't have used that word. You know which word I'm talking about. I won't say it again, and I don't want you to repeat it."

Still staring at her, the children nodded their little heads—even Danny, who surely had no idea what was going on. Then Makayla jumped up and stood in front of Cassie. "Mommy and Darrell used to say that word all the time."

"I know, and so did I, but it's not a good word. So we don't want to use it."

"What happens if we do? Will you shut us in our room?" Makayla asked, her eyes narrowing.

Cassie pulled Makayla into her arms. "No, sweetheart, no one will shut you in a room anymore."

Makayla extracted herself from Cassie's embrace and ran to Wade. "I like you, Mr. Wade, because you didn't lock the door on us when we were bad."

Cassie picked up Danny and walked across the room. Taylor and Jack followed. Cassie tousled Makayla's hair. "You weren't bad. It was all an accident, and I shouldn't have yelled."

Makayla turned and threw her arms around her aunt. "I love you, Aunt Cassie. We won't let you say that bad word again."

"Good. Now let's go to the beach," Cassie said, motioning toward the door.

Cheers rose from the three older children as they raced down the stairs. Still holding Danny, Cassie looked at Wade, relief showing in her smile. Her eyes were bright with unshed tears.

The scene tugging at his heartstrings, Wade smiled back, knowing he'd been pulled much deeper into her life than he'd ever wanted. A young woman with a pretty face had enticed him to accept an invitation to lunch, and his misguided wish to impress her had prompted him to go to the beach with the kids. Now he was being drawn in not only by her outward beauty, but by her determination to make a family for her nieces and nephews.

As much as he longed to let all his emotions take over and pull him in, he couldn't let that happen. It wouldn't be fair to her. She had enough concerns, without him putting himself into the mix. He might consider seeing where his interest in Cassie would lead, but she didn't need a man who could suddenly have a recurrence of a deadly disease.

Yet he thought about Angie's request that he help Cassie, that he be her friend, and about his own promise to help her. How was he going to do that without letting his feelings for this young woman be more than they should be?

Maybe if she kept calling him sir, he'd remember how much older he was. Remember to be her friend and nothing more. But was that even possible, when just watching her interact with the kids turned him inside out? She needed a friend, and that was what he would be. He couldn't count the number of people who had helped him through his battle with cancer. This was his chance to help someone else—to make a difference.

Chapter Four

Makayla darted from the patio into the living room. "Aunt Cassie, hurry up! Mr. Wade's coming!"

Knocking lightly on the window, Wade let himself in. "Ready to go?"

Makayla twirled around the living room. "I'm ready!"

"Me, too!" Jack said, imitating Makayla.

Sitting quietly on the couch, Taylor held Danny in her lap.

"Makayla, Jack, sit still, before you crash into something." Cassie glanced at Wade. "Sorry. I'm almost ready." She stuffed some towels into the beach cart. "I just have to put in some snacks for the kids and a few more toys for Danny."

He crossed the room. "Do you need help?"

"Sure. Grab those bags of baby carrots and juice boxes in the fridge and the box of crackers on the counter." Cassie's heart skipped a beat when he handed her the things she'd asked for.

Trying to ignore the effect he was having on her, she

hurriedly tucked the snacks away in one of the zippered pouches. They had just attended church together for the fourth Sunday in a row. So why was she having this re-action to him now?

She should be used to Wade's presence by now. After that first weekend he'd spent with her and the children, they'd begged to have him help them build a new sand-castle each time they went to the beach. And they'd in-sisted on going to church.

Despite the familiar routine, Wade still made her a little nervous. She was always afraid she would make another blunder like the swearing episode. She tried not to think about the look on his face after she'd let fly with a curse word that she'd used hundreds of times before she became a Christian. He'd seemed to understand, but surely his opinion of her had plummeted.

She tried hard not to curse anymore, but old habits were often there to ambush her. Cursing had been second nature in the household where she'd grown up. She couldn't let that be the case now. The children needed her to set a good example.

Her influence on the children counted much more than impressing some man. She wasn't looking for a man in her life. So that should be the end of thinking about Wade Dalton. But he wasn't easy to forget, especially when he treated her with a respect she didn't believe she deserved.

What would it be like to have a kind man like Wade have a romantic interest in her? Such were the thoughts of someone lost in a fairy-tale world. She had to come to grips with reality. In real life, a refined, well-educated man wouldn't be interested in a redneck woman. When would the impossibility of any romantic relationship with this man soak into her brain?

Cassie carried Danny and followed behind the other children as they helped Wade pull the beach cart across the giant sand dune. When they reached the other side, the children immediately grabbed their buckets and shovels and began digging in the packed sand.

Makayla looked up and placed her hands on her hips. "Mr. Wade, aren't you going to help us build the sandcastle?"

He appeared to stifle a grin as he glanced at the little girl. Cassie was sure his eyes were twinkling behind the sun clips that hid them from view. Her stomach plunged like the pelicans diving into the nearby ocean for fish. Trying to ignore Wade's effect on her, Cassie gazed at the bright blue sky filled with cotton-puff clouds.

"Makayla, we need to help your aunt first. And don't you need some sunscreen?"

"Yes, sir." Makayla nodded her head, then marched over to Cassie. "I'm ready for sunscreen."

Cassie marveled at the way her younger niece wanted to please Wade. And as the children lined up to get sunscreen, she realized she was no different. Pleasing Wade Dalton seemed to have risen to the top of her list.

While Cassie smeared sunscreen on the kids, images of Wade taking charge with them and praying with her, played through her mind. He'd helped her without condemnation. All those things made her want to forget all the reasons she shouldn't complicate her life with a man—even if he *was* wonderful.

The way he smiled, with so much understanding, made her want to throw her arms around him and never let go. The romantic ideas lingered in her mind like the bubbles of foam left on the sand by the retreating waves.

What was she thinking?

She tried to think of something other than Wade as she pulled canvas beach hats of various colors from the cart. "Okay, kids, one more thing. Miss Angie called to remind me that she bought hats for you to wear to help protect you from the sun. Everyone gets one."

"I want the pink one!" Makayla yelled, jumping up and down.

"Okay." Cassie handed the pink hat to Makayla, who twirled it in the air as she ran back to her bucket. "Put it on your head."

Taylor quietly took the green hat, while Jack grabbed the khaki one and pulled it down on his head until his eyes were barely visible. Both kids ran off to join Makayla in the sand, and Cassie found a little blue hat for Danny.

"Where's mine?"

Cassie looked up. Wade stood there with his hand outstretched and a smile curving his lips. She took a deep breath. The man was getting more gorgeous every time she looked at him. How was that possible?

When she first saw him, she'd been unimpressed. But now, every time she looked at him her heart fluttered. She kept noticing how his broad shoulders filled out his T-shirt and how virile his hand looked as he held it out to her. She was tempted to grab hold of it.

Hoping to gain control of her senses, she rummaged through the zippered pouch on the cart. She finally found another hat at the bottom and pulled it out. "It's all yours, if you want to be seen in a hat covered with flowers."

His smile widened to a grin as he took the hat. "At least they're blue flowers." Without another word, he put it on his head and joined the kids, who had scampered away to build their new sandcastle.

Staring after him, she donned her own straw hat and wondered how she was ever going to keep from liking this man too much. A man who could wear a flowered hat without being embarrassed certainly had to be very sure of himself.

She turned her attention to Danny, who stood nearby dressed in bright red swim trunks that hung to his knees. "Play, play." He waved his hands and waddled toward the older children, his cute little feet leaving tiny footprints in the sand.

The image reminded Cassie that the most important thing was to keep these children together. That should be enough to keep her from letting thoughts of romance color the picture. But that realization was hard to hang on to when she saw Wade. Still wearing the flowered hat, he was on his hands and knees, right in the middle of the children, while he helped them shape the beginnings of their castle.

Danny stumbled into the circle they'd drawn for the moat and promptly lost his footing on the uneven ground. He plopped down in the sand on his diaper-padded bottom and smashed two towers of the castle.

"Aunt Cassie, he's ruining our sandcastle!" Makayla wailed, trying to shove the toddler away. "He's going to mess up everything!"

Before Cassie could reach the little boy, Wade scooped Danny up in his arms. "What are we going to do with this one, Aunt Cassie?" he asked with a grin.

The rather serious neighbor she'd met over three weeks ago had been grinning a lot today. And that grin made her heart race. She held out her arms. "Let me take him. I'll see if I can keep him out of the way."

"Here you go."

"Thanks." Their fingers brushed as they made the exchange. The touch sent Cassie's insides on a roller coaster ride. Swallowing hard, she tried to ignore her crazy reaction to this man. *Get a grip.* She quickly averted her gaze and looked at Danny. "Okay, little man, you have to quit being the destroyer."

"Play! Play!" Danny yelled as he squirmed in her arms. "Down! Want down!"

Cassie clutched the wriggling child tighter. For a moment, she feared he'd struggle free and fall. Finally she set him down, and he started toward the other children again.

This time, Wade intercepted him before he reached the newly constructed towers. Grabbing a little blue plastic pail, Wade again carried the little boy to Cassie, but as soon as Wade set him down, the child toddled away on his pudgy little legs. Wade chased after him, and he giggled in delight. The chase had become a game.

"Mr. Wade, don't let him ruin our castle again!" Makayla blocked Danny's path. When he tried to dart around her, she grabbed him around the waist and pulled him to a stop. "You stay away!"

Danny let out a loud wail. Cassie was sure everyone on the beach would turn and look their way. She hurried to assist, but before she got there, Wade picked up another bucket and handed both to Makayla and then scooped Danny up with one arm.

Makayla held up the buckets. "What do I do with these?"

"I'll tell you in a minute. Just wait right there." Wade turned to Taylor and Jack. "I want the two of you to dig the moat on the line we drew around the castle, okay?"

"Yes, sir," they chorused.

Still holding Danny, Wade turned back to Makayla. "Now you and Danny are going to use the buckets to get water to fill the moat."

Makayla started to run toward the surf but stopped and looked back at Wade. "But Danny'll ruin stuff. He's just a baby and doesn't know what to do."

"You can help him."

Makayla wrinkled her little brow and pursed her lips. Then she nodded her head. "Yeah, I think I can do that. I'll show him how to do it right." Grabbing her little brother's hand, she gave him a bucket. "Come on, Danny. Let's fill our buckets with water."

Digging her toes into the soft, wet sand, Cassie watched the scene with amazement. What had happened to the man who had finally admitted to her that he didn't usually care much for the beach? And where had this bachelor learned to deal so well with children?

Makayla and Danny traipsed toward the water's edge. As they drew near the churning surf, Danny hunched his shoulders and refused to move. When a wave came crashing toward him, he dropped his bucket and ran to Cassie as fast as his little legs would carry him. He threw his arms around her legs and clung to her. His bucket bobbed harmlessly in the surf.

"Danny's afraid of the waves, but I'm not," Makayla

announced to Wade in her familiar know-it-all voice. "That's 'cause I'm big and he's a baby."

Retrieving the bucket, Wade filled it with water and looked at Makayla. "Don't you think we should help him not be afraid of the waves?"

Shrugging, Makayla wrinkled her nose. "Maybe." She glanced in Cassie's direction. "Aunt Cassie, what should we do?"

Cassie picked Danny up and walked toward the water. The little boy wrapped his arms tightly around her neck and pressed his head against her shoulder. She recognized the fear in his tense little body. When she joined Wade and Makayla in the shallow surf, she tried to lower Danny to the water.

"No go! No go!" He had a stranglehold on her neck.

"Aunt Cassie, how come Danny's afraid of the water?" Makayla asked.

"Maybe because the waves seem really big to him. They probably look scary."

Makayla stood on her tiptoes and patted her baby brother on the leg. "Danny, you don't have to be afraid. See? I'm in the water. It doesn't hurt."

Refusing even to look, Danny shook his head vigorously.

"Seems as though we're not going to get him into the water today," Wade said, gazing down at Makayla. "Let's take our buckets of water and fill the moat."

"Okay, but Danny wasn't any help, was he, sir?"

"Not today, but maybe he'll help us another day."

"Tomorrow?"

"Not tomorrow. I have to go to work."

"Being a for…ster?"

"Yes."

"Can I go to work with you?" she asked, trying to match his strides.

Glancing at Cassie, Wade gave her a lopsided grin before he turned his attention back to Makayla. "No, I can't take a little girl to work with me."

"But I could help lots. See? I'm helping you now."

"You *are* being a big help, but you're too little to be a forester now. But you can be one when you grow up."

"Yippee! I can be a for…ster. I can be a for…ster," Makayla said in a singsong voice as she skipped ahead, her bucket sloshing water as she went.

Cassie's admiration for Wade continued to grow every time he interacted with her or the kids. He'd encouraged a small child to reach for something big. She needed to remember to do that with the children.

How much better her own growing-up years would've been if someone had been there to tell her that she could be whatever she wanted to be. Still, Angie had come into her life in the nick of time and let her know that she was someone important, especially to God.

Cassie wanted to be as encouraging to her nieces and nephews as Angie had been to her. With God's help—and maybe a little help from a very nice man named Wade—she would do her best to give these kids confidence and a good life.

When Cassie, Danny, Wade and Makayla got back to the sandcastle, Taylor and Jack had completed digging the moat. With shovels in hand, they stood by, waiting for the water to fill the trench.

"Good job, kids. You made a great moat."

Lowering her head, Taylor smiled. "Thank you, sir."

"You're welcome, Taylor." Wade hunkered down and slowly poured water into the little ditch.

"I want to pour water, too," Jack said, clamoring for Wade's attention.

"We're going to need more water," Wade said as most of the water sank into the sand.

Makayla poured the contents of her bucket into the moat and watched most of it disappear, too. "What's happening to the water?"

"It's soaking into the sand," Wade replied.

"Why?" Makayla asked.

Still holding Danny, who now seemed content in her arms, Cassie listened as Wade tackled Makayla's question. She couldn't help thinking of the huge responsibility she had to answer all the questions they'd have in their lives. The thought of what she had undertaken suddenly overwhelmed her. She took a deep breath in an effort to settle her mind.

"Do not be anxious about anything." The phrase flitted through her mind. It came from the Bible, but she couldn't remember where. She didn't even remember the whole verse, which she had probably read recently. Despite her limited knowledge of the Bible, God was still reminding her to put her trust in Him.

"Aunt Cassie, don't let Danny wreck our sandcastle again." Makayla's words brought Cassie's thoughts back to the here and now.

"I won't."

Standing, Wade held out a bright green bucket and plastic shovel to her, while he adjusted his glasses underneath the brim of his silly looking sun hat. Even in flowers he looked good. "You could show Danny how to fill the buckets full of sand. He'd probably like that."

"Okay." Cassie lowered Danny to the ground, breathing a sigh of relief when he didn't immediately dart toward the emerging masterpiece.

She sat on the sand beside him and showed him how to shovel sand into the pail. He caught on to the idea and soon had it filled to the brim. He clapped with glee when Wade turned the bucket upside down and the packed sand became part of the castle wall. The little boy eagerly started refilling his pail with sand.

Cassie helped Danny fill his pail over and over again, and the sandcastle grew bigger and better. Wade sent Taylor and Makayla in search of a small piece of driftwood to serve as a bridge over the moat. Within minutes, they returned with several pieces. After trying each piece, they picked one to do the job.

"Would you say the castle is finished?" Wade asked as he stood and rubbed the sand off his hands and knees.

Cassie hid a smile when she saw Jack mimicking every move Wade made. "I think it looks great."

"Me, too." Makayla clapped her hands.

"But we still need water in the moat." Taylor pointed to the trench that contained barely a hint of water. "There's hardly any left."

Wade picked up one of the nearby buckets. "Okay, kids, grab your buckets. Let's fill up the moat."

"Yes, sir!" the children chorused.

Taylor and Makayla each picked up a bucket, and Jack picked up two. They followed Wade down to the edge of the water. The scene made Cassie think of the Pied Piper. The children were following him as surely as the children in the old tale. She was drawn to follow him, too. She picked up Danny and meandered closer to the ocean, trying to gauge his reaction. He appeared not to care that they were getting closer to the water.

Soon the kids had filled their pails and headed back to the sandcastle. They poured the water into the moat, and, just like before, the water slowly sank into the ground.

"It still didn't work!" Makayla cried. "Now what do we do?"

"Get more water," Wade said.

"Okay!" the kids chorused as they raced with Wade back into the ocean to refill their pails.

This time, when Cassie reached the water's edge, Danny squirmed in her arms. "Down. Down."

She set him on the wet sand near the water to see what he would do. Seemingly without fear, he toddled toward the water.

Wade glanced down just as Danny stepped into the surf. "Well, well, look who's decided to join us." Wade looked up at Cassie with a smile. "Someone isn't afraid of the ocean anymore."

"Yeah, I guess so." Cassie smiled in return, her heart hammering. One look from this man had her thinking impossible thoughts again. Thoughts of romance. Thoughts of family. Thoughts that were dreams.

Big dreams.

But wasn't that what she wished for the children— making dreams come true? Why not for herself? She pushed that thought away before it could settle in her heart. Reality. That was what she needed to focus on.

She quickly turned her attention back to the kids. Makayla was helping Danny fill a pail with water. In minutes the group was headed back to the castle. They emptied their pails of water into the moat, and this time most of the water remained.

"It worked!" Makayla jumped up and down and twirled around. "Yippee!"

As they stood back and admired their creation, a white pickup truck with the words Ocean Rescue painted on the side in bright red lettering stopped nearby. A deeply suntanned young man poked his head out the window. "We're asking everyone to leave the beach."

"What's the problem?" Cassie asked.

"We've received a weather bulletin that severe thunderstorms are approaching from the west. We're trying to get everyone off the beach before they get here."

"Thanks. We'll start packing up. Okay, kids, we've got to go," Wade said with authority as the truck continued slowly down the beach.

"Why…?" Makayla whined.

"Because the man said a storm's coming." Packing the beach cart, Cassie gazed at the peaceful ocean and the bright blue sky overhead dotted with a few puffy white clouds. The weather assessment didn't seem very accurate. Then she glanced toward the western sky, behind the town houses. Ominous dark clouds hovered at the edge of the horizon.

Jack pouted and sat on the sand near the sandcastle. "I don't want to go in."

"Jack, look at those black clouds." Cassie pointed upward. "Those are storm clouds. You don't want to be on the beach when there's lightning. It's very dangerous. Besides, it's nearly four o'clock. We've had enough beach and sun for the day."

"Yeah, Jack, we need to hurry." Taylor gathered the pails and shovels. "You better do what Aunt Cassie says."

In minutes, they had the beach cart packed, and the kids once again helped Wade pull the cart over the dune to the walkover. With Danny in her arms, Cassie followed close behind. When they reached the top of the stairs, a streak of lightning cut a jagged line across the sky. Thunder echoed in the distance.

Cassie quickened her pace. What she really wanted was to cower under something, but she didn't want the kids to know how much the approaching storm bothered her. Ever since she was a kid, thunderstorms had frightened her. She remembered sitting hunched under a mattress in the bathroom of their ramshackle house during a tornado warning. She could still hear the crackle of the little battery-operated radio that had updated the warning until it was safe to go out.

The sky grew darker, and big fat drops of rain began pelting them as they made their way along the walkover. "Hurry, kids. Wait on the patio until I can unlock the door," Cassie called to them as they ran ahead, pails swinging by their sides.

Taylor turned back. "But don't we need to wash the sand off our feet?"

"No, we can't take the time. We can do it on the patio." Cassie turned to look at Wade. Loping along the walkover, he pulled the cart, its wheels clicking across the boards. "Are you doing okay?"

"Yeah. I'm fine. Don't wait on me."

Before Cassie could respond, the rain changed from intermittent large drops into a sheet of wind-driven water. The rain plastered her hair to her head. She tried her best to shield Danny from the downpour as she raced to the end of the walkover. When she reached the patio, the other children huddled against the door under the overhanging balcony that covered the patio. Not even the covering kept the wind-driven rain from soaking them.

Balancing Danny on one hip, Cassie managed to unlock the door. "Go in and stand in the kitchen."

Jack and Makayla hurried into the town house, but Taylor still stood on the patio. "But my feet are all covered with sand. I'll get the floor dirty."

Cassie touched the child's shoulder. "We're not going to worry about that now. We just want to get out of the rain."

When Wade reached the patio, he popped through the door, closed it behind him and gazed back at the patio. "What should we do with the cart? It's getting all wet."

Cassie looked out at the rain, a wall of water obscuring the view of the dunes. She couldn't see the ocean beyond. The sky had darkened so much that it seemed more like night than day. "Forget the cart."

"Mr. Wade, you're dripping all over the carpet." Taylor's soft little voice could barely be heard above the pounding rain.

Wade glanced down. "I sure am. Better get in the kitchen with you kids."

"Mr. Wade's in trouble. Mr. Wade's in trouble," Makayla sang.

"Makayla, that's enough. We don't have time to be silly."

"I think I *am* in trouble." Wade's voice made Cassie turn in his direction. "I lost that hat. It blew off in the wind."

Cassie laughed. "It's not much of a loss. Y'all wait here while I get some towels."

Cassie hurried into the laundry room. She soon returned with an armful of towels and handed them to the three older children and to Wade. She wrapped a towel around Danny and ruffled his hair until it was almost dry.

Wade dried off as best he could, but his clothes were still soaked. "I'd better head home so I can get some dry clothes."

Just as Wade walked to the door, a flash of lightning lit the sky. Thunder crashed. Cassie shrank back into the room and tried not to let her apprehension show. She worried that the kids would realize her reaction and take on her fear, as well. She wanted them to be vigilant about storms but not overly frightened by them. They needed to learn to be cautious but not fearful.

Makayla ran across the room and threw her arms around Wade's legs. "Mr. Wade, you can't go outside now. The lightning will get you."

"She's right. It's probably not a good idea. It's still raining really hard. Maybe we can find something for you to change into. I'll look around."

"I'll be okay. It's only a few yards to my door." He looked down at Makayla and extracted himself from her little bear hug. "I'll get cleaned up. Then I'll come back. Okay?"

Narrowing her gaze, she nodded. "Won't you get wet coming back?"

"I'll use an umbrella. Maybe by then the storm will be over. I'll see you in a little while." Wade let himself out.

With a growing appreciation for Wade's attention to

the children, Cassie watched him race through the rain until he disappeared on the other side of the wall that separated their patios. Standing at the sliding glass door, she wondered whether he really wanted to come back. Or was he just being polite, for a little girl's sake?

As she herded the kids into the bathroom to get them cleaned up, she caught a glimpse of her reflection in the mirror. Her dark hair was matted on her head and hung in wet tangles around her shoulders. She looked completely disheveled—and Wade had seen her that way! But what did it matter? How many times had she told herself she had no business being interested in her neighbor?

Chapter Five

Rain continued to beat against the window as Wade stared at the dunes just beyond the patch of grass next to his patio. The sea oats bowed to the ground in the fierce wind. He wasn't sure an umbrella would be of much use in the wind. But he'd promised Makayla that he'd come back. Did it matter? Wouldn't she understand if he didn't? After all, she hadn't wanted him to go out in the storm in the first place. But *he* wanted to go back—and his reasons went beyond Makayla.

Part of him *didn't* want to go back—the part that feared getting too involved in the lives of these children and their pretty aunt. The kids weren't as much a concern as Cassie. She had his heart and his brain tied in knots, and he'd only known her for a few weeks. It'd been that way since he'd first met her.

Love at first sight. He'd never believed in it. Still didn't. But how else could he explain his fascination with the young woman next door? It couldn't possibly be love so soon, could it? Still, it was certainly *something*. And he wasn't quite sure what to do about it.

Pacing back and forth in front of the door to the patio, he waited for a break in the downpour. None came. Finally, he turned on the TV to check the weather. The entire radar display showed a large green blob, dotted with yellows, oranges and reds indicating strong thunderstorms. There was no break from the storm in sight.

Just then, a streak of lightning rocketed across the sky, and thunder boomed. The TV screen went blank. The digital clocks on the microwave and built-in oven went dark. He flipped a light switch. Nothing happened. The power was out.

His first thoughts were of Cassie and the children. How would they fare without power? It was still daytime, although it hardly seemed like it. The dark clouds roiling above the beach and ocean, along with the constant rain, blotted out most of the light.

He really ought to brave the storm and check on them. It amazed him that in such a short time they'd become such an important part of his life. They meant a lot to him. They weren't just some noisy little kids who lived next door. He really cared what happened to them. And he especially cared about their aunt. There was no denying the effect she had on him.

Searching through the entry closet, he managed to find an umbrella. Then he waited by the door until there was a little break in the storm. The rain had finally lightened up enough that he could see beyond the patio to the beach. Massive, foaming waves crashed onto the sand.

Wade stepped onto the patio, then locked the door behind him. When he opened the umbrella, a sudden gust of wind threatened to turn it inside out. He waited a minute before making a dash to the neighboring town house. In his haste, he didn't look down, and he managed to step into a big puddle on the way. His shoes filled with water. Standing on Cassie's patio, he glanced down at his thoroughly soaked shoes. Thankfully, they were canvas.

When he looked up, Makayla and Jack, now dressed in shorts and T-shirts, were holding the patio door open. "Mr. Wade, you came back." Makayla grabbed his hand and tried to pull him into the room.

"I said I would," he replied, as he extricated himself from her grasp. "But I can't come in until I take off my wet shoes."

"Hurry, or you'll get wet." She clapped her hands together in excitement.

Wade slipped out of his shoes and left them on the patio. "Where's your aunt?"

"She's in the kitchen." The little girl pointed, then threw her arms out from her sides. "The power's out. Now Aunt Cassie can't finish cleaning up all the sand."

Wade looked around for Cassie and found her using a broom and dustpan on the kitchen floor while an upright vacuum cleaner stood nearby.

"Let me hold the dust pan." He hurried into the kitchen and hunkered down to hold it in place.

She smiled at him. "Thanks."

Her smile turned his stomach inside out. He quickly looked down at the dustpan. "Can't vacuum without electricity."

"Yes, sir, you've got that right." She swept the little pile of sand into the dustpan. "At least I got the kids all cleaned up and changed before we lost the power, but I never had a chance to clean up myself. I'm still a mess."

"You look fine to me." Wade wanted to tell her she didn't just look fine. He wanted to tell her she was beautiful, dressed in the aqua cover-up with her damp hair curling around her face and onto her shoulders, but he didn't know how she would take a compliment like that. She was calling him sir again. To her, he was probably just another middle-aged man.

For a moment, he was tempted to reach out and touch those damp curls. He jumped up and emptied the contents of the dustpan into a nearby trash can to keep from doing something stupid. He wasn't sure about anything regarding this young woman, except that she intrigued him and had him off balance. *Way* off balance.

"Do you have any idea how long the electricity will be out?" She looked at him as though he should know the answer.

He wished he could impress her by telling her the exact moment the power would return. "It could be minutes or hours."

"Oh, I hope it's not hours, because it's going to be difficult to fix supper for the kids without it." She glanced toward the patio door. "I hate storms."

"They definitely can ruin a good day." Her tight-lipped expression made Wade wonder whether she was more than just worried. He wanted to comfort her, but again he was fearful of overstepping his bounds. He was letting this crazy attraction fuel dangerous ideas about a relationship with her. He didn't need that, and neither did she.

"I'm hungry," Jack said, pulling on Cassie's arm.

She looked at Wade, then down at Jack, a pained expression on her face. "I suppose you heard us talking about supper."

The little boy bobbed his head up and down in an exaggerated fashion. "Yeah, I want food."

Sighing heavily, Cassie walked around the breakfast bar into the kitchen and opened the pantry door. She stood there for a moment without speaking. Jack and Makayla hovered behind her.

Makayla maneuvered her way in front of Cassie. "What's there to eat in here?"

"I'm still looking."

Wade wondered whether he should make a suggestion. Was this his concern, or would he be intruding where he shouldn't? Finally, he stepped into the kitchen. "If the power isn't out all over the island, we could go out to eat."

Everyone turned and looked at him. Expectation beamed from the three older children's faces. Concern seemed to crease Cassie's brow when Makayla started jumping up and down and pulling on her arm. "Let's go eat at that place where they have the good pizza! Please, please, please!"

Cassie remained silent. She appeared to be considering his suggestion, but she narrowed her gaze when she looked at him. Her expression told him she wasn't happy with his idea. Leaning back against the counter, she gazed at Makayla. "We don't know whether any restaurants have power, so don't get your hopes up."

Makayla stuck her chin in the air. "When will you decide?"

Cassie turned and opened a kitchen drawer. She pulled out a rectangular plastic box and a few coloring books. "I want all of you kids to go into the living room and color while I talk to Mr. Wade."

Makayla grabbed the box and handed it to Jack. Prancing through the kitchen, she waved the coloring books in the air. She stopped long enough to look up at Wade. "Mr. Wade, will you take us out to eat again?"

Wade tousled her hair as she went by. "That's what your aunt Cassie and I are going to discuss."

With anticipation written all over their faces, the children settled on the floor in the living room where some light came in through the patio door. They began to color. Taylor helped Danny, who scribbled with a big blue crayon.

Cassie stepped back around the breakfast bar and surveyed the activity in the living room. "Taylor, please make sure Danny doesn't write anywhere except on the book."

"Yes, ma'am," the girl replied without taking her eyes off her baby brother.

Cassie returned to the kitchen and spoke barely above a whisper. "Taylor's my little helper. I don't know what I'd do without her."

"She certainly seems to like taking care of Danny," Wade replied in an equally quiet voice. "Would you like to explore the idea of going out to eat?"

Cassie released a harsh breath. "I don't know. I can't have you paying for our meal again, and I can't afford to feed these kids at a restaurant, no matter how inexpensive. You've already done way more than—"

"It's okay, Cassie," Wade said, interrupting her. His heart ached when he saw the tears welling in her eyes. "You and the kids have made being here a treat. I've enjoyed every minute. I haven't had this much fun in years. I think God brought you all into my life to cheer me up."

A slow smile curved her pretty mouth. "You really think that?"

"Yeah, I do."

"You've been more help to us than we've been to you."

"I don't know. Maybe God saw that we needed each other," Wade replied, then wondered how far that statement went. He'd let his thoughts wander into romantic territory again, and this wasn't the time or the place. He should be thinking about feeding hungry kids, not wishing their aunt would look at him as something other than the nice guy next door. Hoping to shift his thoughts, he asked, "Got a phone book? I'll call a few restaurants to see if they're open."

Fifteen minutes later, he hung up the phone and turned to Cassie. "Every place I've called has no power. It seems the whole area is without electricity."

Cassie rubbed her fingers back and forth across her forehead. Just as she opened her mouth to say something, another flash of lightning and a crack of thunder punctuated the truth of his statement. With a little gasp, she backed into the kitchen. "I don't think I'll ever get used to that. The lightning seems so bright, and the thunder so loud."

"Maybe it seems that way because we're basically unprotected here at the beach. We're out in the open— no trees to muffle the sound."

"I guess." She turned toward the pantry and opened it again. "I hope I can find something for the kids to eat before Jack starts complaining again."

"You can always feed them cereal. I still have

cereal sometimes in the evening, when I don't feel like cooking."

Shaking her head, she leaned his way and whispered, "No, I've got to come up with something better. That's what Taylor used to feed the other kids when Sam and that bum of a husband of hers were strung out on drugs. Poor little thing was always playing mom to her brothers and sister. I just get furious when I think about how they neglected those kids."

"They had it rough, huh?"

Nodding, she closed her eyes. She steepled her hands in front of her mouth, as if she were trying to gain control of her emotions. When she looked back at him, she managed a little smile that reminded him of Taylor. He saw the resemblance between the aunt and the niece. "They really did. I don't want to do anything that reminds them of that time."

"I see what you mean."

"I just want to gather them close and hold them tight so nothing bad can ever happen to them again. They've been through so much."

Cassie's vehement declaration drew Wade in, making him want to be in that circle, too. A circle full of love and caring. He was beginning to recognize a lot of Christian charity at work here. He wanted to be a part of that love.

He'd had a wonderful family growing up, but in his adult years, he'd been burned by love. Now this young woman had touched his life in a way he'd never expected—in a way he'd never been touched before. He was drawn to her against his better judgment, and it seemed that the only way to keep from caring about her would be to disassociate himself from her and the kids.

And that wasn't going to be possible, when he lived right next door.

"What will you feed them, if not cereal?" he finally asked, trying to force his thoughts in another direction.

She reached in the pantry and brought out a jar of peanut butter. "Peanut butter sandwiches, and we've still got some baby carrots left. And I could probably cut up a couple of apples."

"I'll help fix the sandwiches. Show me where the bread is?"

Cassie looked at him as if he had three heads. "You're going to help?"

"Don't you want my help?"

"Sure, but I've never been around a man who did anything in the kitchen, except Angie's husband before he died."

"Angie's a widow?"

Cassie handed Wade a loaf of bread. "Yes, her husband died suddenly three years ago. Heart attack. Angie took over his construction and real-estate business."

"Sounds like a busy lady."

"I admire her so much. She's my role model." Cassie waved a hand in the air. "And she's made all this possible for me and the kids. She helped me get a job here, too."

Wade took slices of bread from the bag and laid them on the counter. "What kind of a job?"

"Receptionist at an insurance agency." Cassie twisted the lid off the peanut-butter jar and handed it to Wade. "Tomorrow's my first day."

"What will you do with the kids?"

"They'll go to day care. That was all arranged through the social-service agency that handles foster care."

They fell silent as they worked together to make the simple meal. As the children colored, the sound of their voices mixed with the sound of the thunder that continued to rumble, eventually growing softer, each peal coming farther and farther apart.

Wade cut the sandwiches in half and placed them on plates. "Sounds like the storm is about finished. Maybe the power will be back on soon."

"Maybe." Cassie picked up a couple of plates and headed for the table. "Okay, kids, come and eat."

Jack was the first one there. Taylor held Danny's hand as she brought him over. Makayla scrambled to make sure she sat by Wade.

"Mr. Wade, are you going to pray for us again?" Makayla asked.

"Sure." Wade bowed his head and prayed, thinking how grateful he was to God for showing him, through these children and this young woman, how much he had to be thankful for in his life.

While they ate, the rain subsided but didn't stop. A cloudy mist hovered over the dunes just outside the window. Still, the power didn't come back on. After they finished eating, the older kids helped to clean up. Even Jack managed to put his plate in the dishwasher.

"What can we do now? I'm tired of coloring," Makayla whined as she made her way to the living room. "We can't watch TV or anything."

"We can read a book. I'll get one." Cassie started for the bedroom. Before she reached the hallway, a flash of lightning brightened the room, and thunder boomed again, rattling the patio doors.

Taylor let out a little scream, and Makayla covered

her ears. Danny, who sat on the living-room floor, started to cry. Jack didn't seem to care. He started to jump up and down on the couch.

"So much for the end of the storm," Cassie said as she stopped in mid-step and turned back to the living room. She scooped Danny off the floor and patted his back in an effort to comfort him. "Jack, get off that couch. You know better than to jump on it. What would Miss Angie say if she saw you doing that to her nice furniture?"

"Yes, ma'am." Jack sat on the couch and, to Wade's surprise, hung his head. "Please don't tell on me."

"I'll have to tell her if you ruin her furniture."

"I won't do it no more." He sat very straight and pressed his back into the cushion, his little legs sticking straight out and his blue eyes wide as he stared up at his aunt.

"That's good." Cassie motioned to Taylor and Makayla. "Girls, sit on the couch with Jack."

"Yes, ma'am." They raced to sit on either side of him.

Reading the frustration and fear on Cassie's face, Wade fought the urge to draw her into his embrace. Concentrate on the kids. Yeah. That was what he needed to do. "Would you like me to take Danny while you look for a book?"

She glanced at him, almost as if she'd forgotten he was there. "Yes, sir. That would be great."

Wade held out his arms for the little boy, and he went to Wade without a fuss. Looking at Danny, Wade marveled that he was once again taking care of a toddler. He had to admit he was actually getting used to being around *all* of the children. But being comfortable around Cassie was making it difficult not to think of her in romantic terms. He'd been pushing those kinds of thoughts away without much success. How many times would she have to call him *sir* before it finally soaked into his muddled brain that they weren't right for each other?

While he waited for Cassie's return, he set Danny on his shoulders and marched around the living room. The little boy giggled.

"I wanna do that, too," Jack said, jumping up and chasing after Wade and pulling on the hem of Wade's shorts.

"Me, too. Me, too." Makayla joined the parade.

Stopping, Wade looked down at Jack and Makayla. "Not right now. Your aunt Cassie will be back in a moment. I'll give you a ride after we read the story."

Sweet little Taylor continued to sit on the couch with her hands folded. Wade's heart went out to this quiet child, who reminded him of his oldest brother, Peter. He'd been the quiet one in the family, too. Wade, on the other hand, had always been the outgoing, talkative one of the three brothers. Maybe that's why Makayla had taken to him so quickly. They were two of a kind.

Life had been a lark. Everything had come easily to him until the cancer. The events of the past couple of years had changed him, and made him more serious— made him think more about God and about being a responsible person. But he'd also forgotten how to have fun, until he'd moved here and met Cassie and these kids.

When Cassie returned, she sat next to Taylor on the couch. Still holding Danny, Wade found a seat in the chair on the other side of the room. While he sat there, he really looked around at the furnishings in the town house for the first time. Had Angie thought about her nice things when she offered to let Cassie and her charges stay here? How would glass-topped tables, couches and chairs covered in light fabrics, and off-white carpet fare with four little kids running around day after day?

Cassie had her work cut out for her trying to keep the kids from making a mess of things. Maybe that was part of her stress. Was there any way he could help? Not hardly.

As Cassie opened the book, Taylor and Makayla snuggled up to her. She looked from one to the other and smiled. "Are you girls ready for a story?"

"Yes, ma'am," they said in unison.

Jack found a spot on the floor by Cassie's feet and pounded on his chest. "I'm ready, too."

"Good, then we can get started. This is a Bible story about Jesus healing a sick man."

"What was wrong with him?" Makayla asked.

Cassie patted Makayla on the hand. "Well, let's read the story and find out."

Cassie's southern accent gave a melodious sound to the words as she read the story of the man let down through the roof so Jesus could heal him. Even the occasional rumble of thunder didn't distract the children from the story. Cassie had their rapt attention as she read with enthusiasm. Wade could understand why. She had his attention, as well.

Wade let Cassie's voice wash over him. The sweet sound soothed him. Contentment settled around him as Danny fell asleep in his arms. He glanced down at the sleeping child with amazement. Never in his wildest dreams had he thought to find himself in such circumstances. And the funny thing was, he didn't mind at all.

His life had taken another big turn, and he wasn't

sure he was any more prepared for this one than he'd been for the cancer that had threatened his life. This one threatened all his preconceived notions about what he wanted out of life.

Cassie glanced up at Wade as she read the story. He was looking down at Danny, who was sleeping soundly. Her heart did a little flip-flop when she saw this wonderful man holding her little nephew. She hurriedly fixed her gaze on the book again before her mind took her on a fantasy tour of a family that included one Wade Dalton. That kind of thinking was completely nuts.

After Cassie finished reading the story, even Makayla looked sleepy-eyed. "I think you kids need to get ready for bed. We have to get up early tomorrow so Aunt Cassie can go to work and y'all can have fun at day care."

"But I don't want to go to bed yet, and I don't want to go to day care," Makayla said, shaking her head. "Besides, Mr. Wade said he'd give us rides after you read the story. I want a ride like Danny."

Cassie looked over at Wade, who sat there looking like a kid who'd been called into the principal's office. He grimaced. "I'm sorry. I didn't know they were going to bed after the story."

"They don't have to go bed, just get ready."

Makayla ran over and gazed up at Wade. "Can we do rides first, Mr. Wade?"

"That's up to your aunt."

Makayla turned to Cassie. "Please, ma'am?"

Cassie suppressed a smile. Was she being a pushover every time Makayla begged for something? Most of the time, it was hard to say no to her. The responsibility to make the right decision concerning these kids weighed heavily on Cassie. "Okay, as long as you get ready for bed after the rides are over."

Makayla jumped up and down. "Yippee!"

Taylor hopped up from the couch and looked at Wade. "Do I get to have a ride, too, sir?"

"Me first," Makayla said, before Wade could answer Taylor's question.

"Makayla, don't interrupt. Mr. Wade will decide who goes first."

"Okay." Makayla folded her arms across her chest.

"Thanks for giving me *that* decision," Wade said, giving Cassie a lopsided grin.

"Would you like me to take Danny?"

Holding the sleeping toddler, Wade carefully stood. "Sure."

Danny didn't stir as Wade placed him in Cassie's arms. When he smiled down at her, she was sure her heart was beating so loudly that it rivaled the distant thunder. If she weren't holding Danny, she would have been tempted to put her hand over her heart in an effort to cover the sound, even though she knew Wade really couldn't hear it. She mustered a smile. "Have fun."

"I will," he said as she turned toward the stairs.

While she got Danny ready for bed, he barely awakened. A day in the sun had obviously worn him out. Hopefully, the other children would be worn out, as well. But judging from the giggles and laughter coming from the living room, she had her doubts.

Maybe it hadn't been such a good idea to let Wade give them rides. They would get all riled up and not want to go to bed. And if she got them there, they wouldn't fall asleep, because they would be so wired. But she re-minded herself that these kids needed to have some fun. They needed to laugh and play and be kids—especially Taylor. Her seven-year-old eyes had seen too much of the raw side of life already.

Laying Danny in the crib on one side of the bedroom, she wondered whether she should cover him with a blanket. Without power, the air conditioning wasn't run-ning. The rain hadn't cooled things down, just made it more humid. The town house was already beginning to feel a little too warm, especially on the second floor.

She rubbed her hand over Danny's head, which sported very little hair, then leaned over and kissed his cheek. Her heart swelled with love for this little boy. Although he was her sister's child, Cassie was begin-ning to think of him, and the other children, as her own. They were depending on her to make things right—to give them the kind of life every little kid deserved. And she wouldn't fail. God would guide her.

Cassie bowed her head. *Lord, thank you for allowing me to have the kids. Please give me wisdom to make the right decisions for them.*

A loud crash interrupted her prayer. She hurried down the stairs and into the living room. With the chil-dren gathered around him, Wade lay on the tile floor in the eating area, next to an overturned chair.

Cassie halted at the edge of the carpeted area in the living room. *"What happened?"*

Chapter Six

Everyone turned and looked at her, their eyes wide—even Wade's.

Grimacing, Wade sat up, an embarrassed grin on his face. "I tripped."

"Over that chair?" Cassie asked, knitting her eyebrows in a frown.

"Yes."

"Is anyone hurt?"

Adjusting his glasses, Wade sprang to his feet and picked up the chair. "Only my pride."

"Would you like to explain, Mr. Wade?" Cassie tried to act stern, now that she realized no one had come to any harm during all the commotion.

"I can tell you what happened, Aunt Cassie," Makayla said, as if she could hardly wait to explain.

Cassie bit her lip to keep from smiling. "Maybe we ought to let Mr. Wade do that."

Walking over to where she stood, Wade eyed her as if he could read her mind. "Sure. I'll—"

"He was chasing Jack and ran into the chair. The

chair fell over, and he did, too." The high-pitched words tumbled from Makayla's mouth as if she would burst if she didn't tell on Wade. "He shouldn't have done that, right, Aunt Cassie? He might ruin Miss Angie's stuff."

A smile still threatening to curve her lips, Cassie raised her eyebrows and looked at Wade. Then, to keep from bursting into laughter, she hurriedly turned her attention to Makayla. "I thought we were going to let Mr. Wade explain."

Makayla put her hands on her hips. "But he didn't see it. I did."

"Well, next time, don't interrupt." Cassie gave her niece a reproving look.

"Yes, ma'am." Makayla pressed her lips together and crossed her arms over her chest. "Is Mr. Wade in trouble?"

"I don't know. I need to hear his explanation." Cassie glanced at Wade, and this time she smiled. "What do you have to say for yourself?"

"Ah…well, I'm sorry I got carried away playing with the kids. The rides turned into a game of tag. We should've saved that game for outside. Sorry."

"I accept your apology." What had happened to the completely serious man who hadn't even wanted to go to the beach the day they first met? Now he was roughhousing with the kids? Had she completely misjudged him?

"Thanks. It won't happen again." A lopsided grin slanting his mouth, Wade stared at Cassie. "Are we forgiven?"

"Yes," Cassie replied.

"Well, now that I've caused enough trouble, I'd better get going. Sorry to wear out my welcome." Grimacing again, Wade backed toward the patio doors.

"It's okay, really." Cassie didn't want him to go away feeling bad. She liked his less-serious side even more than the serious one—and that was tempting enough.

As Wade started to open the door, a flash of lightning skittered across the darkening sky, accompanied by a crack of thunder. Pouring rain suddenly starting pelting the patio.

Wade jumped away from the door. "Wow! Maybe I won't go."

"Aunt Cassie, don't make him go. He said he was sorry. I didn't mean to get him in trouble." Makayla hurried to block his exit.

"Makayla, honey, please come away from the door." Cassie reached for the child and pulled her close, then glanced at Wade. "You really shouldn't go out in the storm."

"I only live next door. It's not like I have a long way to go." He motioned toward the three children, who were now all gathered around Cassie. "Besides, you have to get the kids ready for bed."

Cassie gazed out the window at the storm, which had seemingly subsided but was now gaining new strength. She didn't want to be in the storm alone with the kids. How could she let Wade know that without frightening the children? In fact, how could she get him to stay without telling him she was terrified of storms? She was probably more afraid than the children. She finally turned her attention back to Wade. "Please don't go."

"Yeah, Mr. Wade, don't go. You could spend the night with Aunt Cassie. Then she won't get lonely," Makayla said, smiling up at the two adults.

"Mr. Wade will leave when the storm is over," Cassie said, her cheeks burning.

Makayla surely had no idea what she was saying. But who knew what these kids had been exposed to while they lived with two adults who were under the influence of drugs or booze most of the time? She didn't dare look at Wade. What must he be thinking?

Cassie wished *she* had somewhere to go. Maybe lightning would strike and open up a hole in the floor. She'd gladly fall into it. Getting the kids ready for bed would rescue her from Makayla's embarrassing suggestion.

"Okay, kids, time to get ready for bed."

"Not yet," Makayla moaned.

"Yes, yet." Waving her hands and trying to avoid Wade's gaze, Cassie tried to shoo the children up the stairs.

Taylor's little giggle filled the air. "Yes, yet," she repeated. "That's funny."

"Yes, yet. Yes, yet. Yes, yet," Makayla mimicked as she marched around the room.

"You'd better quit being silly and do what Aunt Cassie says, or you'll be in trouble just like Mr. Wade," Taylor said, heading upstairs to the bedroom. "I'm going to be ready for bed first."

"No, you won't. I'll be the first one ready. And Mr. Wade's not in trouble anymore!" Makayla shouted, racing to beat Taylor.

Jack charged after them. Smiling and shaking her head, Cassie dared a glance at Wade. "Nothing like a little competition to get things started."

His hazel eyes twinkling with laughter, Wade shook

his head. "Seems as though Makayla has wiped my slate clean. I sure hope her aunt has done the same."

"Chances are good." Cassie turned away quickly and went after the children, in order not to let those twinkling eyes make her pulse race.

She waylaid Jack before he went into the bedroom where Danny was sleeping. She put her finger to her mouth to show that they had to be quiet as she slowly opened the door. "You wait out here while I get your pajamas."

Jack nodded, putting his finger to his mouth in imitation. After getting Jack's pajamas, she helped him change in the bathroom, so they wouldn't disturb Danny.

When she came out of the bathroom, Wade was lounging against the wall in the hallway. "Do you want me to take Jack while you help the girls? We promise to be good."

His grin made her stomach do that familiar flip-flop. The feeling took her back to middle school and her crush on Billy Washburn. She was grown up, with grownup responsibilities, but she felt like a young girl with her first crush. "No tag this time?"

"No tag. How about a piggyback ride?"

"As long as you manage to stay on your feet." Cassie couldn't help laughing. In fact, she was feeling downright giddy.

When she arrived in the bedroom, Makayla had already discarded her clothes in a heap on the floor and put on her nightgown. Cassie noticed for the first time how frayed and discolored the gown was. At least it was clean now, not dirty and smelly, as it had been when she brought their things from the filthy mobile home where they were living. The thought of that place made her shudder.

She wished she had the money to buy them new things, but she knew things didn't bring happiness. Makayla was happy with her faded pink nightgown, because it was clean. And she had a clean bed to sleep in.

In her typical fashion, Taylor laid her clothes neatly on the bed as she took them off. "Aunt Cassie, what should I do with my stuff?"

"Is it clean?" Cassie asked, not wanting to wash the threadbare clothes any more than she had to. She feared they would fall apart if she did.

"I think so."

"Okay, then put them in the drawer in the chest. Makayla, if yours are clean, you should do the same."

"Yes, ma'am." Makayla raced to take care of her clothes.

When Cassie and the two girls returned to the living room, Wade and Jack were lying on their stomachs. They were both coloring. Cassie had never seen a grown man coloring. The sight touched something deep down inside her.

Here was a man who didn't depend on macho activities to show his masculinity. The way he treated these kids showed him to be more of a man than any she'd ever known. It said a lot about his character.

Running to join them, Makayla grabbed one of the coloring books from the end table beside the couch. "Mr. Wade, I didn't know you liked to color."

"I do." He looked up at her. "Would you like to join us?"

"Yes, sir." Makayla plopped down next to Wade and opened her coloring book.

Not to be left out, Taylor got another book and found a spot on the floor next to Jack. The scene reminded Cassie of the way the kids had followed Wade at the beach. It was another Pied Piper moment.

She continued to stand there until Wade glanced up. "You don't like to color?" he asked.

She shrugged. "I just haven't done it in a long time."

He motioned to her. "Well, come on down and get in on the fun. There's a spot right here." He scooted over and patted the open space between him and Makayla. "You can fit in right here."

"There aren't any coloring books left," Cassie said, thinking how much she'd like to fit into Wade's life.

"We can share."

"Sure." The look he gave her made her weak in the knees. She sank to the floor before they gave out. Trying to regain her equilibrium, she took the crayon he offered her without looking at him, for fear he might see how much all this was affecting her. "Thanks."

The two adults and three children lay spread out like the spokes of a wheel, with the coloring books the hub. Cassie tried to concentrate on the picture of the fire truck she was coloring, but all she could think about was how she and Wade were lying nearly shoulder to shoulder in the tight circle. And she kept thinking about how virile his hand looked as it held a crayon. Nothing, not even the lightning and thunder, seemed to keep her from noticing everything about this man.

The sound of thunder grew more distant again, but the ping of rain on the windows didn't abate. As the thunder subsided, Jack fell asleep with his head lying on one page of the coloring book and a crayon still in one of his little fists. Cassie didn't disturb him, and the rest of the group continued to color until the light began to fade.

Finally, Cassie stood and whispered, "I'm fixin' to put Jack in bed. You girls can keep coloring until I get back."

The girls nodded without looking up from their books.

Pushing himself up until he was kneeling, Wade whispered back, "Do you need help?"

Cassie shook her head and carefully lifted Jack. She carried him up to the bedroom, where Danny was still sound asleep, despite the storm. When she returned, Wade was sitting on the couch while the girls continued to color.

"Okay, girls, it's time for you to go to bed, too."

"I want to finish my picture," Makayla said.

"It's getting almost too dark to see. You can finish it tomorrow."

"But tomorrow we have to go to day care."

"That's true, but you can finish it tomorrow night."

Taylor closed her book and put her crayons in the box. "Will you read us a story before we go to sleep?"

Cassie looked at Taylor with surprise. She hardly ever made requests. Makayla was the one who was always making demands. How could she turn Taylor down the first time she asked for something? Cassie glanced around the room in the waning light. "Taylor, sweetie, it's almost too dark to read. Maybe if we can find a flashlight or candle, we can read a story. Let's see if Miss Angie has any candles."

Cassie searched the kitchen until she found two jar candles sitting on the top shelf of the pantry. She couldn't reach them, even standing on her tiptoes.

Wade came up behind her. "Did you find something?"

Cassie pointed to the shelf. "Yeah, right there. Can you get them?"

Without waiting for her to get out of the way, he reached over her head, brought one down and handed it to her, then got the other one. When she turned around, he was standing so close that she was sure he could hear her heart pounding. He smiled down at her, and she forgot to breathe.

In an instant, he turned away and went in to the other room. She stood there staring after him. He obviously wasn't feeling the same connection she was. Why should he? After all they'd only known each other for a few weeks. But in those weeks, she'd seen more to like about this man than she'd seen in any man she'd known in years. His kindness toward the children made him worthy of admiration. And she reminded herself that she should stop with admiration. That was as far as her feelings for this man should go.

Taking a deep breath, she gathered her wits and went into the kitchen in search of matches. While she looked, Makayla raced into the kitchen. "Aunt Cassie, I remember where I saw a flashlight."

"Where's that, sweetie?"

"In the garage." Makayla raced to the door that led to the garage.

"Hold on!" Cassie set the candles on the counter and chased after the little girl. Cassie managed to stop her before she opened the door. "It's going to be dark in there. You won't be able to find a thing."

Wade came up behind Cassie. "You'll be able to see if you go to the car and open the door. The dome light will give you enough light to see."

Turning, Cassie smiled at him as she tried not to let his nearness affect her again. "Good idea. You wait here, Makayla, until there's some light. Then you can show us the flashlight."

Once there was light in the garage, Makayla ran right to a flashlight plugged into an outlet on the garage wall. "Here it is." She pulled it out, but no light shone from it. "Why doesn't it light?"

"Let me see it," Wade said, and Makayla handed him the flashlight. He pushed the prongs that had been in the outlet, then pushed another button, and the light came on.

"How'd you do that?" Makayla asked, jumping up and down trying to see.

Wade hunkered down next to her and showed her exactly what he'd done. "Do you see how it works now?"

"Yes, sir."

After they came back inside, Cassie used the flashlight to search the kitchen for something that would light the candles.

"How about this?" Wade held up a long-handled lighter, then flicked the trigger. A flame came out the end.

"Perfect," Cassie replied, holding out the candles.

Wade lit them, and Cassie set them on the snack bar that separated the living room from the kitchen. The flames flickered in the jars, giving a soft glow to the room.

While Cassie read, Makayla held the flashlight and Taylor turned the pages of the book. Cassie tried to focus her attention on the story, not on Wade, who sat in the nearby chair. But whenever she glanced up, he was sitting there smiling at her. Each little look sent sparks through her midsection as powerful as the lightning outside. She was in more trouble than she'd thought. No matter what he was doing, she was too aware of him. When she finished reading the story and closed the book, she forced herself not to look his way. "Okay, girls, it's time to go to bed," she said.

Taylor immediately jumped up from the couch and Cassie prepared herself for Makayla's protest. But the little girl surprised Cassie by joining her sister without complaining. Both girls headed for the bedroom, but Makayla stopped midway up the stairs and ran back to where Wade sat. Taylor came running back, too.

Makayla tapped Wade on the arm. "Mr. Wade, thank you for taking us to church and helping us make a sandcastle."

Wade smiled. "You're very welcome. Thank you for inviting me to be part of your day."

"This was the best day ever. You made it fun." Taylor's quiet little voice barely sounded above the rain that still beat against the window.

"Thank you," Wade replied.

Cassie glanced at Taylor, who lowered her head, a little smile curving her lips. The child had echoed Cassie's thoughts. Despite the storm, it *had* been the best day ever. "Okay, no more delay. Off to bed."

Wade stood. "Good night, girls."

"Good night, Mr. Wade." Makayla skipped away, but then stopped and turned. "You don't have to go. Aunt Cassie will let you stay with her."

Cassie wanted to fan herself to relieve the heat creeping up her neck and face. Maybe the reason for her warmth was the lack of air-conditioning, but she suspected it was the embarrassing conversation. She'd dismissed the subject earlier, but Makayla didn't want to let it go.

"Makayla, we've already said Mr. Wade will be going home soon. Now get going." Cassie hurried the girls up the stairs, glad for the dim light that hid her flaming cheeks.

After Cassie said prayers with the girls and tucked them into bed, she stood just outside the bedroom door and wondered how she was going to face Wade when she came back.

She plodded back downstairs with the flashlight illuminating her way. If only she had something to illuminate her thoughts and show her how to deal with Wade.

This was the first time they would be together without the children as a buffer. That scenario wouldn't be so bad if not for Makayla's very embarrassing comment. Could God help in a situation like this? She was only starting to learn to lean on Him. Did God get tired of hearing her requests? Angie said no, but a heavenly Father was hard to understand when her earthly father hadn't been a very nice man.

When she reached the living room, Wade was standing with his back to her. He appeared to be gazing out the patio doors at the thunderstorm that continued to rage. The candles still flickered in the jars, making the light dance on the walls and ceiling. Then a streak of lightning lit up the darkened sky, silhouetting Wade. He held an umbrella in one hand. Was he preparing to leave, despite the downpour?

The thought of holding an umbrella in a lightning storm made her shiver. She didn't want Wade to go out under these conditions. It was too dangerous, even for a short distance. Besides, deep down inside, she didn't want him to leave, because she wanted company to help her ride out the storm. What would his reaction be if she asked him not to go? Makayla's remark might have made him wary. But surely he realized the child didn't understand the meaning of what she had said.

Taking a deep breath and straightening her shoulders, Cassie determined to make the best of the whole situation. She wanted some adult conversation that didn't include children. She missed having time for herself. After dealing with her nieces and nephews, she had a growing appreciation for single parents.

"Well, the kids are in bed," she said, ready to face whatever might come.

Turning, Wade gave her a lopsided smile and stepped away from the doors. The flicker of the candlelight reflected in his glasses, so she couldn't read the expression in his eyes very well. "That's good. I should probably head home."

Cassie glanced toward the patio doors and the torrent that still battered the building, dunes and beach beyond. She had to convince him to stay. "You don't want to go out in that, do you?"

He turned to look out again. "Not really. I noticed my shoes are full of water. And your beach cart is pretty soaked," he added with a chuckle.

"Water won't hurt that cart or anything in it. I'm sorry about your shoes." She grimaced and hoped she could convince him to stay. "Don't go. I promise to let you leave as soon as the rain lets up. I won't hold you captive or make you stay the night, as Makayla suggested." She was trying to make light of the situation, and she hoped she was doing a good job.

When Wade didn't say anything, she wanted to slink

away in embarrassment. He didn't think her comment was funny. Now what should she say?

Then he chuckled, his attention still focused on the outdoors. "That Makayla is a corker. It was all I could do to keep from laughing when she told me you'd let me spend the night."

Cassie laughed, too, relief washing over her. Even though Wade understood, she felt her cheeks growing hot again, and she put her hands against them. "Oh, I'm so glad you're laughing. I was so embarrassed. I didn't know what you must've thought."

"I kind of guessed maybe overnight guests were the norm when she was living with her mother."

"You do understand." Cassie put her hands over her heart. "I shudder to think what those children may have seen. I only wish I'd been there for them sooner. If I'd only visited more often, I might've saved them from all that. But I didn't like my sister's husband. I felt really uncomfortable the two times I went there, once after Jack was born and again right before Danny was born."

"Did you suspect the drug use then?"

"Not from Sam. I thought her husband was a boozer, but then my daddy was, too, and we all survived."

"You mentioned before that the kids lived in filthy conditions. Didn't that bother you when you visited?"

"Mostly I thought it wasn't any of my business." Cassie frowned, wishing she'd been more concerned back then. "Anyway, things didn't seem that bad when I was there. The place was a little messy, and the kids' clothes were a little dirty. I thought it was mainly because my sister had just had a baby or was just about to give birth. Sam was never the best housekeeper, and her lazy husband never lifted a finger to help. I tried to help out, but I always felt like I was in the way. I was just glad to leave."

"What about your parents? Weren't they concerned?"

"My parents…" Cassie hesitated. Did she really want Wade to know what a sorry background she came from? Oh, well, he had probably already guessed most of it. There was little point in trying to salvage her image. Maybe that thought would put to rest the crazy notion that somehow this very upstanding man could have an interest in her. She'd come to the conclusion that he liked helping people. He probably looked on her and the kids as a project, and she had the suspicion Angie had prompted his participation. Nothing like being a charity case. "You probably wouldn't understand parents who don't do their best by their kids."

"You might be surprised. Even parents who are trying to do their best with their kids don't always do the right thing."

"Oh, that's a given." Cassie motioned toward the couch. "If you're planning to stay for a while, let's sit down." She hoped she wasn't suggesting the wrong thing.

Wade grinned. "I thought you'd never ask."

"Would you like a glass of iced tea?"

"Sure."

Cassie hurried into the kitchen and managed to find the pitcher of iced tea in the dark refrigerator. She grabbed a few ice cubes and quickly closed the door so as not to let too much warm air into the freezer. She prayed that the electricity would come back on before the food was ruined. Spoiled food wouldn't help her budget.

As she brought the glasses of iced tea into the living

room, Wade sat on the couch, his face lit by the candle-light. How had she ever thought he wasn't handsome? He was more attractive every time she looked at him.

As she handed him the glass of tea, she was careful not to let their fingers touch. With the candlelight flickering throughout the room, she was having a hard enough time keeping her romantic notions at bay. Any contact was sure to spark more thoughts of romance—something she didn't need to complicate her life right now.

He took a drink of his tea, then peered at her in the dim light. "So, what were you saying about your parents?"

Cassie sighed. "Too many kids. Six of us. Too little money. And too much booze. That made for a frightful time while I was growing up. I could hardly wait to get away. I would've dropped out of high school and gone out on my own if it hadn't been for Angie."

"Did you go to live with her?"

Cassie shook her head. "No, but I spent a lot of time at her house, and people from her church invited me to spend time with them, too. That's when I began to see what being a Christian was all about. It took me awhile, but finally I wanted what they had. I wanted that peace in my life. I wanted to know I could rely on someone bigger than myself. You know what I mean?"

Wade didn't say anything for a minute, then finally nodded. "But being a Christian isn't always the easy way."

"Yeah, I…I know that, but it's a lot better than living the way my family did."

"What about your other siblings?"

Cassie wondered why Wade was so interested in her family. Did he really care, or was he just being polite? Maybe he wanted to see whether the rest of her family was as messed up as her sister. "Besides my sister Samantha, I have three older brothers and one a year younger than me. They're all in the armed services and have lived all over the U.S. and the world. I rarely see them."

"Have they had to fight in any of the recent conflicts?"

"Yes, but right now, thankfully, they're all stationed in areas where there isn't much fighting. I pray for them every day."

"I understand the worry," Wade said, releasing a heavy sigh. "My brother Matt was in the National Guard, and he was severely wounded while he was in Afghanistan."

"How's he doing?"

"Better, but he still walks with a limp."

"I'm so sorry."

"Thanks. Tell me your brothers' names, and I'll pray for them, too."

"Tom, Harlan, Jeremy and Scott. Thank you," she said, feeling terrible about her cynical thoughts concerning his questions. He had personal experience with the worry. He was a Christian who cared about people. Hadn't she seen that in the way he interacted with the kids? She didn't want to talk about herself anymore. She should find out about him. "Tell me about your family. You're so good with kids. You must have lots of experience with children."

Wade chuckled. "Not really. In fact, to be honest, kids usually make me uncomfortable."

"They do?"

He nodded. "Probably because I was never around them much. I'm the youngest in my family. I have two older brothers."

"No nieces or nephews?"

"Nope. My brothers are single, too. We keep getting engaged, but we never make it to the altar."

"Why's that?"

"I guess we just aren't very good judges of women. We keep picking the wrong ones. Or maybe we just don't know how to hang on to a woman."

"You were engaged?"

He nodded. "But it's been over for a while."

"Why did you break your engagement?"

"I didn't. She did." He looked away, as if he didn't want to talk about it anymore.

"I'm sorry. That was rude of me to ask." Why had she asked such a blunt question? Had she said too much? But why would any woman give up a man as good as Wade Dalton? Did he have some flaw that Cassie didn't see?

After all, if she looked at it honestly, she hadn't known him very long and knew little about him. Despite all the good things she'd seen in this man, she needed to caution herself about getting too interested, for so many reasons, not just the fact that she barely knew him.

The questions still rained in her mind like the storm outside. She longed to ask every one of them, but that would be worse than what she'd already said. She needed to remember that time often revealed the truth about people. And she still had a lot to learn about Wade Dalton.

Chapter Seven

Wade could read the curiosity in Cassie's eyes. She definitely wanted to know about his broken engagement. Thankfully, he could tell by her apology that she wasn't going to ask anything else. He didn't want to talk about the hurt, the disillusionment or his fight with cancer. He just wasn't ready to share. Maybe he should. Cassie had shared things from her past with him. But she probably looked on him as almost a father figure—someone she could confide in—especially since her own father hadn't been much of a role model.

He shrugged. "That's okay. You shared your troubles with me. Life often throws bumps in our path."

"That's why I'm so glad I have Jesus in my life."

"That's a good thought." Wade hadn't always trusted in God the way he should. The cancer had brought him to his knees and made him seek a renewed reliance on God.

"But even though I know God is with me, I'm glad you're here, too. Thanks for staying. I needed the company. Makayla was right about that." The words tumbled out of Cassie's mouth as if she were embarrassed to admit she wanted his company.

"Why?"

"Because storms scare me. I didn't want the kids to know. I don't want them to be afraid like I am."

"Why are you so afraid?"

"When I was a kid, there was this really bad storm, a tornado. It didn't hit our house, but one of our neighbors lost theirs. Storms just make me remember how scared I was." Cassie sighed. "I try to tell myself I shouldn't be afraid, because God is there no matter what, but that old fear lingers. I know God's in control. I even see His power in the storm."

"Especially tonight," Wade said, waving his hand toward the window. "Did you see the waves before it got dark?"

Cassie nodded and flinched when another flash of lightning brightened the room. Thunder boomed, accenting the steady sound of waves crashing onto the beach. "When I look at the waves and see how huge they are, I think of Jesus calming the storm. That must've been something for the apostles to see! I try to think of that story when I get frightened."

"You said you haven't been a Christian very long, but you seem to know a lot of Bible stories."

"Yeah, I've read a lot of stories to the kids from that Bible story book. And besides, when I accepted Jesus as my Savior, I just wanted to read and read and read the Bible." Cassie smiled. "I just love Jesus! Because of Him, I'm free from all the bad stuff that used to surround me. I'm forgiven, a child of God."

"Yes, you are," Wade replied, moved by her expression of love for Jesus. Had he ever made such a free and open declaration of his love for the Savior? He couldn't remember ever doing so. Yet Cassie proclaimed her love with such fervor. Even though she'd stumbled in her walk with God when she swore at the kids, being in her company today had reminded Wade more than once of some important truths. God loves. God forgives. God protects.

Suddenly there was a beep, and the digital clocks on the oven and microwave began to blink their blue numbers.

"The electricity's back." Cassie sprang from the couch and tested a light switch. "We have power!"

"Yes, we do." The bright light made Wade squint as he watched her twirl around the room. Her excitement was contagious. Her presence and enthusiasm for life gave him a boost. Right now, even if she was to call him sir again, he would feel younger than he'd felt in a long, long time.

"It's just a relief. I'd better reset the clocks." She looked at him. "Do you know the correct time?"

He glanced at his watch. "Nine twenty-three. Since the lights are back on, I'll head for home."

She punched in the correct time. "Yeah, I suppose you should, since the rain has let up, too."

Wade couldn't ignore the disappointment that zipped through his mind when she was so agreeable about his leaving. What had he hoped—that she would beg him to stay again?

Lights back on, no storm, no need for Wade Dalton. Where was his head? He knew with a certainty that no romantic thought about him had crossed her mind. So why was he disheartened? He needed a reality check. Going to his own place would give it to him.

"Thanks for including me in your day."

Cassie placed a hand over her heart. "I should be the one thanking you. You helped us so much."

"It was my pleasure." Picking up his umbrella from the floor, he couldn't shake the thought that their conversation was too polite, too stilted. But why, after they'd spent so much time together today? Could it be that she was suddenly feeling uncomfortable, for some reason? Was she feeling embarrassed about revealing her fears and her past to someone she really didn't know that well? After all, he'd been rather tight-lipped about his own fears and his own past.

He pushed open the patio door and stepped out. Picking up his shoes, he dumped the water out of them and groaned. "Guess I'll be going home in my bare feet."

Cassie flipped on the outside light and followed Wade out onto the patio. "Sorry about your shoes. Wow! Hear that ocean. I don't even have to see it to know the waves must be huge. The sandcastle is definitely gone. I just hope the kids won't be bugging me again all week and asking me when they can build another one. They ask where you are every day, and whether you're going to help them build a sandcastle."

"You can tell them sandcastles are reserved for the weekend."

Cassie laughed. "Like that's going to satisfy them."

"Well, you can always try."

He gazed into the darkness as he stepped off the edge of the patio. His bare feet sank into the wet grass. A warm, humid breeze rustled the sea oats. Clouds raced across the quarter moon. He pointed toward the sky. "Look. It's starting to clear. You can see the moon, and some stars."

Cassie looked up. She stood silhouetted against the light illuminating the patio. The breeze ruffled her cover-up around her knees. Wonder showed on her face as she gazed at the sky. "It's incredible. God's creation."

"It is."

They stood side by side for a few minutes. They said nothing as they stared out at the ocean that still roared with angry whitecaps. Gripping his shoes and umbrella, Wade fought the urge to put an arm around Cassie's shoulders and pull her close. It would be so easy to let his feelings for her get out of control. He should say good night.

Taking a deep breath, he made a move toward his town house. "Well, thanks again for the nice day. I'd better call it a night. I've got another big week ahead of me, and so do you."

"Yeah. Say a little prayer for me that I'll do good on my job. I want to do my best, so Angie won't be disappointed she got it for me."

"Sure," he said, thinking that her determination to do well would carry her through, but a little prayer would always help. "And please say one for me, too."

"I will."

"Good night, Cassie."

"Good night, Mr. Wade," she said with a giggle. "That was for Makayla."

Wade laughed out loud. "And I can hear her saying it, too. Have a good week."

"I will." She waved and went back inside.

Wade walked the few feet to his own patio, but he didn't go inside. He lingered there, still taking in the sounds around him. A dog barked in the distance, and the buzz of cicadas accompanied the rhythmic roar of the ocean.

One incredible day had made him reassess his plans. The thought of going back to his empty house wasn't inviting, after spending the day with the chaos of four kids and one pretty woman. To think, he'd come here for solitude, and now he didn't want it. Solitude was the last thing on his list.

Late that Friday afternoon, Wade gazed at the flat landscape of Northern Florida as he rode in George Casper's gray truck. Stands of pine trees lined the road for miles. The smell of well-used equipment and the outdoors permeated the inside of the truck. This was the part of the job Wade liked best—field work. He loved the outdoors, and he'd missed this kind of work more than he realized. When he'd been dealing with the cancer, he'd spent so many days after his treatments too weak to accomplish much more than a little paperwork in the office. He treasured this new beginning.

After their final stop, George drove back toward the interstate. He chatted about his family—wife, children and grandchildren. Wade could tell his coworker was a real family man. When Wade thought about families these days, he thought about Cassie and the kids.

He wondered how they were doing. The entire workweek had passed, and he hadn't seen them once. Most days this past week, he'd gotten home very late in the evening, and he'd been sure the children were all in bed. But even on the days when he came home at a reasonable hour, there had been no sign of the children next door.

He'd sat out on his patio, hoping they would pass by on a trip to the pool or the beach. And he hadn't tried to kid himself. His vigil centered mainly on seeing Cassie. But he wavered back and forth between wishing to see her and not wanting to see her at all. Part of him wanted to discover whether the attraction was real. Part of him felt that not seeing her was for the best, because his fascination—real or perceived—wasn't something he should pursue.

During the week, thoughts of her had never been far from his mind. While he watched the news on TV in his lonely town house, he wondered what was happening next door. Only a wall separated him from the object of his ruminations. What was happening on the other side of that wall? Were the kids sleeping? Was Cassie watching TV or reading her Bible? His thoughts were more turbulent than a ship tossed about on the ocean.

"You have plans for the weekend?"

George's question complicated Wade's ruminations about Cassie and the kids. Would he see them? Would they go to church with him again? Would they have any contact at all? Wade pushed away the questions. "Nothing other than church on Sunday."

"Nice to hear you go to church. That's an important part of the week for my family. You have family nearby?"

"No, my parents live in Atlanta. I have a brother who lives in Atlanta, and another one in South Dakota."

"Y'all sure are spread across the country. I'm thankful all my family's right here in the Jacksonville area."

"I used to live in Atlanta before I took this job."

"So had you visited the island before you moved here?"

Wade shook his head. "Never had the opportunity, although the couple who rented me their town house told me it's a wonderful place to live."

"They're telling you the truth. You're going to love it here," George said with a smile. "Since you're new to the area, let me give you some suggestions about things to do besides going to the beach."

"What's that?"

"Have you been to Fort Clinch?"

"No. There's a fort here?"

"Yeah, it's an old Civil War fort. It's located in a state park at the northern tip of the island. Great place for camping, hiking and picnicking. Lots of cool history stuff. My grandkids love to visit."

"Sounds like an interesting place. I'll consider giving it a try," Wade replied, wondering about the possibility of taking Cassie and the kids to the fort. Then he asked himself why every scenario was dotted with thoughts of four little kids and their aunt.

After they arrived back at the office, Wade hurried through his reports. It had been a long time since he'd been this eager to get home. When he got there, he intended to visit with his neighbors. Waiting around until they bumped into each other by accident wasn't accomplishing anything. He was going to go over tonight and knock on their door. He was done torturing himself with waiting and hoping something would happen. He was going to make it happen.

On the way home, he stopped at the grocery for a few items he needed if he intended to eat something besides cereal. Front and center, just inside the doors, was a display filled with every need for the beach—sun screen, beach towels, beach balls, beach chairs, bags of brightly colored plastic pails and shovels, flip-flops, sunglasses, bodyboards and skimboards, air mattresses and inflatable toys.

The bodyboards caught his attention. He wondered whether the kids might like to have some for the beach. He'd seen other kids riding the waves last weekend. What would Cassie say if he showed up with them? When he finally left the store with his food items, he had three different colored bodyboards and an inflatable boat and life vest for Danny in his grocery cart.

A knock sounded on the patio door. Hurrying into the living room, Cassie wondered why Angie and the kids would go around to the patio instead of coming in through the garage. When she saw Wade standing on the patio, her heart skipped a beat. He smiled as she made her way toward the door. She smiled back, wishing she wasn't wearing her oldest pair of shorts and a ratty tank top. Why was the thought of talking to him making her break out in a sweat, when she'd spent an entire evening talking with him without even a hint of nervousness?

All week she'd done her best to avoid running into him—not that he'd exactly been seeking her out. As she reflected on their talk the night of the storm, she wished she could go back in time and undo their conversation. She'd revealed way too much. But he'd been so easy to talk to, she'd babbled on about all her family troubles. What must he think? And what could he possibly want now?

As she opened the door, she tried not to think about how handsome he looked in his khaki shorts, tropical-print camp shirt and sandals. He looked like he should be on the cover of a tourist magazine. His glasses sported the familiar sun clips, so she couldn't read the expression in his eyes, but his smile eased her nervousness.

"Hi. Can I do something for you?" Cassie cringed inwardly. That hadn't sounded very welcoming. Why did he have to have her brain tied in knots so she couldn't even give him a proper greeting?

"Sure. I wanted to ask you something." He glanced past her into the town house. "Where are the kids?"

"Angie came swooping in a little while ago and took them for ice cream, even Danny. She's a brave lady," Cassie said with a chuckle. "She said I needed a break."

"She's probably right. That was nice of her."

Cassie stepped out onto the patio and closed the door behind her. "That's an understatement. Was that what you wanted to ask about? The kids?"

"Well, sort of. It's a nice evening. If you're not busy, would you like to join me for a walk on the beach while we talk?"

Cassie stared at him. Why was he asking her to take a walk, when he could just as easily ask his question right here? Could he actually have an interest in her? She shook the speculation away, not wanting to read anything into his request. "Sure. Let me get my sunglasses."

"Okay. I'll wait right here."

Cassie hurried into her bedroom and glanced in the mirror. Her hair was a wild riot of curls—so unruly in the humidity. But there was no time to fuss. And he'd probably notice if she changed her old tank top and shorts for something better. Grabbing her sunglasses, she vowed not to get overly excited about his invitation. He was just being neighborly. He wanted to talk about the kids. This didn't have anything to do with her personally.

When she returned, the sea oats were dancing on a gentle breeze. Wispy clouds looked like white brush strokes against a blue canvas. The peaceful scene belied any hint of the frightening storm they'd endured last Sunday.

Standing with his back to her, Wade looked toward the ocean. She had the strange urge to run up behind him and throw her arms around his waist. Trying to disregard the crazy impulse, she took a moment to write a note to Angie in case she got back before she and Wade returned. She hoped the task would give her time to regain her common sense before she did something she'd expect Makayla to do. Children often expressed their emotions freely, without regard to the consequences. Adults, on the other hand, had to weigh their reactions at every turn.

Finally she stepped out on the patio and closed the door and locked it. "I'm ready."

He turned at the sound of her voice. "Great. Let's go."

They traversed the short distance to the walkover without talking. Cassie worried about what to say to him. Maybe, after the way she'd run off at the mouth the other night, saying nothing would be an improvement.

When they got to the walkover, he stopped and looked at her. "It's low tide. A perfect time for a walk on the beach."

"You're right. The beach looks so big when the tide's out." Cassie hurried to match Wade's long-legged pace as he traversed the walkover.

"How was your week? Did everything go okay with your new job?"

"Yeah, it's a good job. The people I work with are super nice, and so helpful. And they made me feel really welcome. It's a lot easier than being a waitress."

"Is that what you did before you got the kids?"

"Yeah. The tips were sometimes good, but you couldn't always count on them. And the hours *weren't* good. Too many nights. I couldn't do that with the kids."

"I can see that."

Cassie realized she'd been letting her mouth run again, going into way more detail than she needed to answer his questions. She should've remembered to ask him about his job, rather than going on and on about hers. "How was *your* week?"

"Busy. We did a lot of timber cruising."

"What's timber cruising?" she asked, hoping she didn't sound too ignorant. The term made her think of her teen years, when she'd ridden around her grandma's little town in Georgia with the hottest boy in the hottest car.

"We take sample plots in a forest stand to determine the volume and value of the timber. Then we use a GPS unit to map the area and determine the acreage."

Digesting his explanation, Cassie felt inadequate to respond. If she'd had any doubts the man was brainy, this conversation would have wiped that thought away. The whole thing sounded really complicated. Who knew so much was involved in being a forester?

He stopped at the end of the walkover, where a set of stairs led to the beach, and shaded his eyes with one hand. "Do you suppose we might find that flowered hat?"

Cassie scanned the dunes on either side of the walkover. "Probably not. That was a bad storm."

"In that case, I'll have to buy Angie a new one." Wade started down the stairs.

"Oh, I don't think she'll miss it."

"I should still replace it." He waited for her to go ahead of him on the narrow path that went over the big dune.

Once on the other side, Cassie took off her flip-flops and dug her toes in the soft sand. She gazed out at the expanse of packed, wet sand between them and the water's edge, where waves spilled peacefully onto the beach. What a contrast to the night of the storm.

Wade bent down and took off his sandals. When he straightened, he asked, "Which way do you want to walk?"

"I always like to walk with the breeze in my face on the way back. Seems cooler that way."

"And how do we determine that?"

"Look at the way the sea oats are bowing. That should tell us."

Wade glanced toward the dunes, then turned back to her. "I can tell better by looking at the way the breeze is blowing your hair." He reached out and touched several strands that blew across her cheek, then quickly dropped his hand away, as if he'd been stung by a jellyfish. Turning away, he started down the beach. "Looks like we'll be heading toward the Ritz-Carlton."

"You're right. The breeze is definitely at our backs now." Pushing her hair behind her ears so it wouldn't blow in her face, she hurried to catch up to him and wondered why he had suddenly turned away. For an instant, when he had brushed the hair from her cheek, she'd sensed a spark of interest. Or had she imagined it? Was it just wishful thinking?

Without looking at her, Wade walked toward the surf and let the waves wash over his feet. "How did the kids do this week at day care?"

Cassie walked just on the other side of him, her feet

sinking into the wet sand. "They were good. That's why Angie took them for ice cream. It's their reward."

"I was surprised not to see them all week."

"I didn't want to let them stay up too late or get too wound up before I put them to bed. Otherwise, they get cranky, and even though the day care center is nice, it makes a long day if they're tired. And I knew if they saw you—especially Makayla—they'd get excited." Cassie clamped her mouth shut. Too much information again. She was probably boring him to death and maybe even insulting him with that last statement. She had a nervous need to fill the silence. She wanted to impress him, but she was probably talking his ear off instead, and making him think she thought he was a bad influence on the children.

"Good thinking. I guess I did get them a little riled up the other night, with the roughhousing. Sorry about that."

"Oh, no, I didn't mean it that way. I just meant they get keyed up and don't want to go to bed when there's company."

"I understand."

"Good."

While they walked along, Cassie vowed to enjoy the sights and sound of the beach and the company of this very thoughtful and generous man without talking. The less she said, the better. She had already managed to put her foot in her mouth.

Seagulls gathered in groups along the sand and flew into the air when Cassie and Wade approached. A few joggers dressed in shorts, T-shirts and running shoes ran by them, leaving footprints in the sand. A few yards ahead, an older couple moseyed hand-in-hand and occasionally stopped to pick up a shell and put it in a plastic bag. What would it be like to grow old and still be as much in love as that couple? Cassie had no clue. Her parents certainly weren't a testimony to marital harmony. She had caught a glimpse of it with Angie and her husband, but he had died while still a young man, leaving a grieving wife. Cassie couldn't even imagine the heartache.

In the distance, the Ritz-Carlton Hotel stood in muted tones of brown and tan against the blue sky. A few guests from the hotel still romped in the surf or relaxed on lounge chairs under the row of blue beach umbrellas. The luxury and beauty of the first-class hotel reminded Cassie that only her reliance on God had brought her from the depths of a very troubled family to this island paradise.

Despite the wonderful sights on the beach, Cassie kept thinking about the kind man who was walking beside her. Keeping silent gave her too much time to think about Wade. Had he missed them during the week? Was that why he'd asked about the kids? She had to stop caring about what he thought. She had a great friend in Angie, a good job and a relationship with God. So why did she want to mess that all up by getting interested in Wade?

Finally, she couldn't keep quiet any longer. "You know, of course, when the kids see you, they'll want you to help them with another sandcastle. You've given yourself a permanent summer project."

Wade chuckled. "I hadn't thought of it that way, but I don't mind."

"I hope the kids don't wear out their welcome with you."

"That won't happen. They're too entertaining." Stopping, Wade turned to look at her. "In fact, I bought something for the kids today. That's why I asked you to go for a walk. I wanted to talk it over with you and make sure it was okay with you before I gave it to them."

Cassie's heart sank. So that was what he wanted to ask her. He *had* said his question concerned the kids. So why was she so disappointed? Stupid question. She shouldn't be trying to fool herself into thinking she didn't want this walk to be about her. It wasn't. His interest was in the kids. She mustered a smile. "What did you get them?"

He pointed toward some children playing in the surf. "You see those things the kids are riding?"

"Yeah. Bodyboards? Is that what you got them?"

Wade nodded. "I figured Taylor and Makayla were old enough to use them, but I thought Jack would feel left out if I didn't get him one, too. Is that okay?"

Cassie shoved away her disappointment. She had to be happy he thought enough of the kids to buy them something she couldn't afford. "Thanks. The kids will enjoy them."

"I also got Danny a little boat. And some stuff for the pool."

"Wow. You didn't have to buy so much."

"But I wanted to." Wade laughed. "When I walked into the store and saw all that beach stuff, I immediately thought about your kids. I couldn't help myself. I can hardly wait for the look on their faces when they see everything."

Cassie stepped into the surf and let the waves roll over her feet and the sand slide out from under them. Her hopes of having Wade take a romantic interest in her slid away, as well. His interest lay only in the children. It was just as well. She tried to convince herself of that. Hadn't she told herself all along not to get interested in this man? "You probably won't just see happy faces. You'll hear some loud voices, too, especially Makayla's. When do you plan to give them the bodyboards?"

"That's up to you. I can do it tonight or wait until tomorrow."

"Tomorrow. I think the ice-cream trip is enough excitement for one day," Cassie replied, wondering how bad she was to be using the kids to ensure that she would see Wade tomorrow.

"Okay. Would you like for me to help you teach them how to use the boards?"

"Sure. That would be a big help."

"Tomorrow morning, then?"

Cassie grimaced. "Um…can't do it in the morning. Angie's coming over again to help me put child safety locks and other safety stuff on everything in the town house. We have to get ready for the visit from the caseworker, but I wanted her to be the one to put the stuff on the cabinets. She tells me they have stuff that doesn't have to be screwed on now. So I hope it works."

"Do you need some help?"

Trying not to let her eagerness show, Cassie smiled. "Okay. And you can come for lunch, too."

"I wasn't trying to get a lunch invitation."

"Even if you weren't, you should stay for lunch. We can go to the beach with the bodyboards in the afternoon."

"Sounds like a plan. And speaking of plans, are you going to go to church with me on Sunday?"

Smiling, Cassie nodded. She wished the invitation were something personal. But when it came to church, she should be thinking about God, rather than Wade. "Yes. Thanks for asking."

"And after church, would you be interested in a picnic?"

"On the beach?"

"At Fort Clinch. A guy I work with was telling me all about it. It sounded like something the kids would enjoy."

"Oh, yeah. I forgot about Fort Clinch. I went there once when I a kid. I haven't been there in years."

"Well, it's time you went again."

"Okay, but let's head back. Angie's probably there with the kids by now." Cassie turned around and hoped Wade hadn't guessed how glad she was that he'd offered to help and to take them to church. Maybe if they spent more time together, he would finally see her as something more than the kids' aunt. Maybe he would finally see her as a woman. But would he like what he saw?

Chapter Eight

Water sprayed from the faucet at the end of the walk-over as Wade waited his turn to wash the sand from his feet. Cassie washed off her flip-flops, then held a leg under the shower. He forced himself to look at the sand dunes, the sky, the nearby buildings. He just shouldn't be thinking about the shapely legs of this young woman. He shouldn't be thinking about her at all. So why had he placed himself right in her path by buying gifts for the kids?

The question was easy enough to answer. He *couldn't* quit thinking about her.

What madness pushed him to think about another relationship, after the last woman he'd loved had turned away at the first sign of trouble? Wouldn't other women do the same thing, especially women as young as Cassie? What was driving him to find out? And what kind of sorry excuse for a man used kids to get to a woman? A desperate one. He didn't see any other way to attract her attention. The troubling questions continued to stick in his mind like the sand clinging to his feet.

To make matters worse, he'd almost overstepped his bounds earlier, when he had pushed her hair from her face. He certainly didn't want to scare her away. He still battled with himself over whether he should even pursue a relationship with her. He kept remembering that his health history should make him steer clear, but her enthusiasm for life made him feel so alive. He could listen to her talk endlessly. Her sweet southern drawl was like a siren's song. He loved the way she talked, giving every detail. He didn't want to give that up.

Was that selfish? He hoped not.

"Your turn." Her statement made him look in her direction.

She slipped on her flip-flops and stepped away from the spraying water. She smiled at him, and the smile turned him inside out. That kind of reaction did nothing to detour his possibly wrongheaded idea about pursuing her.

While she waited nearby, he hurriedly washed sand from his feet and legs. If only all the crazy notions about Cassie could be washed away as easily. He turned off the water and joined her as they made their way to the town houses.

Makayla came charging across the grass to meet them, her flip-flops slapping against her heels. "Aunt Cassie, Mr. Wade, look what we got!"

"Whoa! Slow down, or you'll trip and fall," Cassie said, catching Makayla in her arms. "Show me what you've got."

Makayla opened her little hand to reveal a trinket. "Miss Angie bought it for me. We all got something."

"That's nice." Cassie leaned over to inspect the trinket. "Did you get ice cream, too?"

"Yes, they all got ice cream. Can't you tell by the dribbles down their shirts?" Angie asked as she carried Danny outside to meet them. Taylor and Jack tagged along behind.

Cassie looked up. "Makayla came charging at me so fast I didn't notice."

"It melted too fast. So it dripped." Taylor pulled on the front of her shirt, then looked up at Cassie. "Are you mad?"

Putting an arm around Taylor's shoulders, Cassie pulled her close. "No, sweetheart, we can just throw it in the wash. It'll be fine."

"She was afraid you'd whup us," Jack said, showing off the spills on his shirt, seemingly reassured that a whupping wouldn't take place.

Taking in the exchange between Cassie and the kids, Wade remembered that first day, when Jack asked if Wade was going to give them a whupping. The scenario reminded him of all the responsibilities Cassie had undertaken. And here he'd been thinking only about himself, and what he wanted. He had to think about what was best for her and these kids. Could that possibly include him? How was he supposed to know?

Makayla tapped him on the arm. "Mr. Wade, where have you been? I missed you. Are you going to take us to church again?"

Makayla's question put his focus where it should be, on God. Why had he forgotten to include God in his decisions? Why hadn't he made this a matter of prayer? Probably because he hadn't wanted to get an answer that wasn't what he hoped for.

Wade glanced down at Makayla and smiled. "I missed you, too, Makayla. And I'll take you to church every Sunday, if you want."

"Yippee." She jumped up and down. "Then can we go for ice cream again?"

Wade patted the top of Makayla's head. "Can't answer that one."

"I think we're going to deal with one day at a time." Cassie looked in his direction. "We won't talk about Sunday until it gets here."

Wade nodded as he realized Cassie didn't want to overload the kids with too much information, especially the overexcited Makayla. "Okay by me."

"Come see what else Miss Angie bought." Makayla grabbed Cassie's hand, then looked at Wade. "Come on, Mr. Wade, you can come, too."

"Okay, I'm coming." Wade followed the procession of four children and two women, glad for Makayla's invitation.

The light inside the house seemed dim compared to the bright light outside. When his eyes adjusted, Angie disappeared through the door leading to the garage. When she reappeared, Makayla and Taylor were helping her push what looked like a very fancy stroller. He'd never seen anything quite like it.

"I figured you could use this when you go for walks on the beach. It has room for two, so Jack can ride, as well as Danny." Angie stopped in the middle of the living room.

Cassie put a hand over her heart. "You didn't have to get me that."

"No, I didn't, but I wanted to." Angie walked over and

put an arm around Cassie. "You're like a daughter to me, and I want to do everything I can to help you with the kids."

Cassie's eyes sparkled with tears. "But you've already done so much."

"Come on. Try it out." Angie picked up Danny and put him in the stroller, then glanced around the room and motioned to Jack. "The other spot's for you, Jack."

The little boy scrambled to take his seat. Cassie buckled them in, then made a loop through the living room and kitchen. Taylor and Makayla pranced behind as they tried to help.

"That was fun. Let's go for a walk outside," Makayla said, jumping up and down. "Taylor and I can help you push."

Cassie's eyebrows knit in a little frown. "It's getting late."

"Not that late. There's plenty of daylight left. We're right near the longest day of the year," Wade said, then regretted interfering when Cassie's frown deepened. He should've stayed out of the conversation.

"What do you mean by the longest day of the year?" Taylor asked in her quiet little voice.

Wade gazed at Taylor. How was he going to explain to a seven-year-old the science dictating the length of the daylight? Now he really wished he'd kept his mouth shut. But he'd been hoping to prolong his time with Cassie, even if it meant sharing that time with the four children, and Angie, too.

Simple. Keep it simple. That was what he had to do. He hunkered down next to Taylor. "Somewhere around June twenty-first, there'll be more minutes of daylight than on any other day in the year."

Makayla stuck her nose almost under Wade's face. "Why?"

For a moment, he wanted to say *just because,* but he resisted the temptation. He had to think of some easy explanation, just to make a good impression. "Because the sun stays in the sky longer."

"Why?"

Wade considered going into some fancy scientific explanation that the kids couldn't begin to understand, to try to stop the questions. Then he had an idea. They might not understand it, but it might be fun.

Wade stood and looked at Taylor. "Go get your beach ball."

Taylor hurried into the garage and returned with her red, white and blue beach ball. "Here, Mr. Wade."

"You keep it and hold it like this." He placed her near the patio door and adjusted the ball in her hands. "Stand right there. We're going to pretend this ball is the Earth." Then he pointed to Makayla. "I want you to stand in the middle of the room. You're going to pretend to be the sun."

"I get to be the sun! I get to be the sun!" Makayla chanted as she took her place.

"Makayla, that's enough." Cassie tapped her lips with one of her index fingers.

Wade motioned to Cassie. "I need the flashlight we used the other night."

While Cassie went to get it, Jack planted himself right next to Wade. "What do I get to be?"

"Ah…the moon. You can be the moon. Stand next to Taylor," Wade replied, congratulating himself on his quick thinking.

After Cassie returned with the flashlight, he set up a

demonstration of how the sun shines on the earth as it travels around the sun. The kids had a great time, the ladies applauded, and Wade took a bow, then had the kids take one, too.

Makayla bounced the ball around the room. "That was fun. What can we do next?"

"Put the ball away and take that walk before it does get too late," Cassie said.

Soon they were out the door and on their way. Taylor and Makayla assisted Cassie as she pushed the stroller down the street, toward a group of patio homes just past the swimming pool. The sun barely showed above the tops of the gnarled live oaks, with hanging Spanish moss that resembled old men's beards.

While the girls had Cassie skipping ahead, Angie waylaid him. "Thanks for taking me up on my request to help her out. You're great with the kids."

Wade took Angie's compliment, just glad she was there to distract him from Cassie. Even though he had wanted time with her, the way he was beginning to feel had begun to scare him a little. He didn't have any business being this interested in a woman so soon after meeting her, especially a woman as young as Cassie. "Thanks. It's been a different experience for me. I haven't been around kids much."

"You could've fooled me."

Wade chuckled. "Well, I think I got a crash course in kids last weekend. Did Cassie tell you how we rode out the storm?"

"She did. That's one of the reasons I wanted to thank you." Angie glanced at him, then back at Cassie. "I know how frightened she is of storms, and I was worried about her being all alone with the kids and no power. I guess I worry a lot because she's taken on a big, big job. The kids can be a handful."

"As far as I can see, she's doing great."

"I'm glad to hear it, especially since the caseworker will be visiting again next week. Everything went fine with the first visit."

"Yeah, she did mention the next caseworker visit would be soon."

"She hasn't said so, but I've sensed she's very nervous about it."

"What happens when the caseworker visits?"

"They inspect the home to see whether it's a safe and healthy environment for the kids. They look at stuff like the safety locks, fire extinguisher, fire alarm, the yard, food in the refrigerator. They just make sure the home is good for the children. They'll visit for about an hour and also talk to the kids by themselves."

Wade let out a low whistle. "No wonder Cassie's nervous. You never know what Makayla's going to say."

Angie chuckled. "We'll have to make *that* a matter of prayer."

"Mr. Wade, Miss Angie, hurry up. You're getting behind." Makayla stood with her hands on her hips.

"There's a prime example," Wade said, thinking about all the things Makayla could talk about, such as the roughhousing the night of the storm or her mistaken idea that he could spend the night. He'd better start praying now!

The next morning, Cassie lay on the floor, coloring with the kids, to keep them out of the way while Wade helped Angie install the safety locks. Thankfully, Wade hadn't told the kids about the bodyboards, or she'd be fielding questions every five minutes about how soon they'd get to use them. His kindness toward the kids continued to melt her heart.

"Done. We're all done." Angie's voice made Cassie glance toward the kitchen. Throwing the packaging in the trash, Angie motioned to Cassie. "You want to try them out?"

"Sure." Cassie jumped up and walked into the kitchen. She tried not to look at Wade while she opened every cabinet and drawer. "A few of these are going to take a little practice to open."

"So the question is, will these keep the kids out or just the adults?" Angie said with a chuckle.

"I just want them to pass with the caseworker." Cassie tried several drawers again, opening them with more ease.

"I'm sure they'll be fine." Angie picked up her purse from the table and glanced at her watch. "Well, I'm headed back to Jax. I have a house to show."

"I thought you were staying for lunch."

Angie waved her hand as if she were erasing something in the air. "That's what I thought when I first made plans to come out, but this showing came up. So off I go. Y'all have a good time this afternoon at the beach."

"I'm sorry you have to go." Cassie tried to convince herself of that fact. She *was* sorry to see Angie go, but she was also pleased. Now she would have Wade to herself. Silly, silly thought. When would she learn to temper her wants?

"Me, too. Come on, kids. I gotta have hugs before I go." Angie held her arms out wide.

The three older children raced to give Angie a hug. Danny waddled over, and she picked him up and gave him a big, loud smooch on the cheek before she headed for the door. "Y'all be good for Cassie."

Then she shook hands with Wade and thanked him for his help. They only shared a handshake, but Cassie felt a little twinge of jealousy. She berated herself for envying her friend, but she wanted to be like Angie— smart, confident and gracious. Could she ever live up to her mentor's standards? Not if she didn't get rid of these negative and unchristian emotions. Being a Christian wasn't always easy. It required a whole new way of thinking.

"All right. Let's wash up for lunch." Cassie steered the kids into the bathroom.

"You want me to do something?" Wade called after them.

Cassie poked her head out into the hallway. "Just get out some plates and glasses, please."

"I'm right on it."

Watching him retreat toward the kitchen, she wished somehow she could impress him the same way Angie did. But that might never happen. Wade and Angie came from the same world, where people were educated and knew exactly what to say and when to say it. She was just an unsophisticated girl, trying her best to make her way through a complicated world.

After the children washed their hands, they all went down the hallway. Cassie made a promise to herself that she would cherish Wade's help and friendship and wouldn't long for more.

When they reached the kitchen, Wade was struggling

to open the cupboard door. He turned and looked at her as the kids noisily found seats at the table.

Grinning sheepishly, he pulled and poked at the safety lock. "How do you get these things open?"

When she saw that grin, all her promises and vows took wing like the seagulls flying over the beach. "You should know. You installed them."

"That's the problem. I installed them, but I never tried to use them." Laughing, he leaned against the counter. "Are you going to give this dunce some help?"

"I hardly think being unable to open a cabinet with a safety latch makes you a dunce." Cassie picked up Danny and put him in his high chair, then walked into the kitchen.

While Cassie demonstrated how to operate the safety latch, she realized *she* was the dunce, for thinking she could somehow consider this man as only a friend. There was no fighting the attraction.

"Show me that again," he said, standing right behind her.

He was so close that Cassie feared he could hear her racing heart. She hoped her hand wouldn't shake as she showed him how it worked again. When she finished, he reached out to give it another try. Their hands brushed as he pushed on the safety latch and the cupboard opened. Trying to avoid any more contact, she grabbed some plates and shoved them at Wade. "You can put these on the table."

As he took the plates, he gazed into her eyes. "Anything else you want me to do?"

She forgot to breathe, when the only answer to his question that came to mind lingered on the tip of her tongue. *Kiss me.* She pressed her lips together for fear she would really say it.

When he didn't look away, time seemed to stop. Her heart beat faster, if that were possible. Was he really looking at her with admiration, and maybe something more, or was she just wishing that it were so?

Forcing herself to glance away, she turned toward the refrigerator. "You can get the glasses, and I'll get the drinks," she said, hoping her voice would sound normal.

Finally, she took a deep breath and spent a minute calming herself while she rummaged in the refrigerator. What she thought would be a chance to regain her equilibrium, failed to materialize when she bumped into Wade, who was standing directly behind her. He grabbed her shoulders to steady her, and she nearly dropped the jug of milk. She put her free hand over her heart.

Her voice came out in a squeak. "I didn't know you were there."

"Sorry, I didn't mean to scare you."

"That's okay," she said, scurrying out of his grasp. "You can get the plate of wraps out of the fridge."

After she and Wade came to the table, he gave thanks for the food. Then Cassie cut several of the wraps into smaller pieces for the kids, offered one to Wade and took the last one for herself. The whole time, she tried to avoid looking directly at him. Did he have any idea how he was affecting her? She couldn't let him know.

While they ate, Wade entertained the kids with a couple of stories. She was thankful his interaction with the children took his attention away from her. With everyone eating, talking and laughing, Cassie soon forgot to be self-conscious.

"Aunt Cassie, I really like these things. Can you make them again?" Makayla popped another piece in her mouth.

"I'll make them again in a few days."

Gazing at her, Wade raised his eyebrows. "You made these? They *are* very good."

"You seemed surprised. Did you think all I could cook was mac and cheese from a box?"

"No. I just didn't know when you had time to make them."

"Early this morning."

"I'm finished." Makayla jumped up from the chair. "I'm ready to go to the beach."

Cassie gently grabbed one of Makayla's arms. "Hold on. You have to put your plate and cup in the dishwasher and then put on your swimsuit."

"Yes, ma'am." Makayla hurried to complete her tasks. Taylor followed and helped Jack with his plate and cup.

As the kids hurried off to put on their swimsuits, Wade downed the last of his iced tea. "Very good. I hope I'm invited to lunch the next time you make these. Was that broccoli you had chopped up in there?"

Cassie held up her hand to shield her mouth and whispered, "Don't say that too loud. I don't want the kids to know there were veggies in the wraps. It's one way to sneak them in."

"Good thinking. You're a tricky one, aren't you?" Laughing, Wade got up and went to the patio door.

"Yes." It felt good to kid with Wade without feeling so unsure of herself. The little hint of praise boosted her confidence. Boy, was she pathetic.

"Bring the kids over to my place in a few minutes, and I'll give them the bodyboards, okay?" He slipped out the patio door.

"Okay," she called after him.

She plucked Danny from his high chair and carried him upstairs, where the other children had almost finished changing into their swimsuits. The bedroom looked liked a trash heap. What else could she expect? That was the way they'd lived their whole lives, surrounded by filth and clutter. She had to be patient as she taught them to pick up after themselves.

"Okay, girls, before we can go to the beach, you have to fold your clothes into a neat pile on the bed. Then you've got to go back into the living room and put away the coloring books and crayons."

"Yes, ma'am," the girls chorused as they scurried to obey.

"Jack, pick up your clothes and come with me."

"Yes, ma'am."

With Jack following close behind, Cassie carried Danny to the boys' bedroom. She was grateful that, despite the atrocious living conditions they'd endured under their mother's care, she had taught her kids to be polite. Or maybe they were too scared to be anything else.

While Cassie changed Danny's diaper and put on his swim trunks, Jack tried to put his clothes in a neat pile on his bed. When Cassie saw the little mound of clothes he'd made, she was about to tell him to do a better job. But she bit back her criticism when she saw him smiling and standing like a little soldier, so proud of what he'd done.

She had to remember he was only three years old. No one had ever taught him what to do with his clothes. Feeling misty-eyed, she rushed over to him and gave him a big hug. Danny toddled over and gave Jack a hug, too. The scene almost brought her to tears, but she blinked them back as the girls came charging into the room.

Cassie swallowed the lump in her throat and released a harsh breath. "Ready for the beach?"

"Yes, ma'am," the three older children replied in unison. Danny just clapped his hands and smiled.

"Well, let's head over to Mr. Wade's place. He's got a surprise for you."

"What is it?" Makayla asked, hurdling down the stairs.

"You'll see when we get there."

Makayla ran out the patio door. "I'm going to see what it is now."

"Makayla, you need to wait on the patio, and we'll walk over together."

"Okay," Makayla said, hardly able to hold still.

While Cassie gathered their things for the beach, she realized her mistake in telling the kids about the surprise. Slowly she was learning how to handle different situations, but it took work to know what was the right thing to do. And it took work to know how to deal with her handsome neighbor.

Chapter Nine

The clamor of voices and footsteps told Wade that Cassie and the kids had arrived. Hurrying across the room, he marveled at how much he enjoyed being around this noisy bunch. By the time he reached the door, Makayla and Jack had pressed their little noses to the glass and were peering inside. Carrying Danny and dragging the beach cart, Cassie pulled the two youngsters away from the window.

Wade opened the door. "Hi. Come on in."

Stepping inside, Cassie grimaced. "Sorry about the kids making a mess on the window. I made the mistake of telling them you had a surprise for them."

"No problem." That was the truth. There didn't seem to be any problems when Cassie was around, other than how he was going to deal with his growing attraction to her. She brightened his day more than he liked to admit. Neither dirty windows nor noisy kids could take away the good feelings she inspired.

"Mr. Wade, your house looks just like ours, except the furniture's different." Makayla ran down the hallway and started snooping through the rooms.

"Makayla, come back here. You can't go wandering around Mr. Wade's house." Cassie scurried after the little girl and stopped her in the hallway.

Makayla stuck out her lower lip. "But I wanted to see who else lives here."

"Mr. Wade lives here by himself," Cassie told her.

"That must be lonely. You should come and live with us," Makayla said to Wade. "Then you won't be so lonely." She looked to Cassie for confirmation. "Can he live with us?"

Wade read the discomfort in Cassie's stance as she looked at Makayla. "Mr. Wade doesn't need to live with us. He has his own place right here."

"But he's all alone."

"Yes, but he can visit us any time he wants."

Narrowing her gaze, Makayla turned and looked at Wade. "How come you don't have any kids?"

"I'm not married."

"You could marry Aunt Cassie. Then *we* could be your kids."

Cassie pressed her fingers against her forehead as if she were fighting a headache. Then she looked at her niece. "Makayla, Mr. Wade likes his life the way it is. Stop trying to rearrange it."

Taking in the lively exchange, Wade wondered whether Cassie's statement was true. Did he like his life just the way it was? He had thought so, until four little kids and one young woman came storming into his peaceful life.

"Cassie, don't worry about Makayla. She has good intentions." Chuckling, Wade put his arm around Cassie's shoulders and breathed a silent sigh of relief when he felt her relax. He leaned closer and whispered, "I can show her the rest of the town house to satisfy her curiosity, if you don't care. That might steer her mind in another direction."

Shrugging, Cassie gave him a halfhearted smile and whispered back, "Okay. I just didn't want her to be rude."

"She's okay," Wade said, giving Cassie's shoulders another squeeze, glad that she didn't seem uncomfortable with his attention. Then he motioned to the other kids. "Come on. I'll show you the rest of the place."

"When do we get to see our surprise?" Jack's little voice echoed in the stairway.

Surprised it wasn't Makayla who was asking the question, Wade stopped the procession. "When we finish our tour."

Makayla grabbed his hand. "Let's hurry."

With Cassie taking up the rear, Wade led the children around the town house until they'd viewed every corner. When they were back in the living room, he gazed at their eager faces. "Are you ready for the surprise?"

"Yes, yes!" Makayla bounced on her feet and clapped her hands.

"Okay. Everyone line up right here." Wade pointed to a spot where the carpet in the living room ended and the tile of the kitchen's eating area began. The children raced to the spot. "Wait right here. Turn and face the table. Put your hands over your eyes. *No peeking.* I'll be right back with your surprise."

Wade went into the garage and got the bodyboards. When he returned, Cassie, still holding Danny, was standing guard over three fidgeting children.

"Can we look now?" Makayla asked, barely able to stand in one spot.

"Not yet." He lined the bodyboards up against the couch. "Don't move from the line, but you can turn around."

Makayla clapped and jumped up and down. "Bodyboards!"

"Can I have the green, yellow and blue one with all the flowers?" Taylor asked.

"Your aunt will draw out the name of the person who gets to have first pick." Wade held out a bowl to Cassie.

She pulled out a paper and opened it up. He tried to tell whose name she'd drawn by her expression. He suspected the first choice wasn't going to belong to Taylor. After her request, he wished he'd gotten all the bodyboards in the same color. But he'd thought different colors and designs would give each of the kids a distinctive board. Then they wouldn't argue over whose was whose.

He found that dealing with kids was a learning experience in just about every situation. Even though both Cassie and Angie had told him he was good with the kids, he wasn't sure that was the case. He wanted to help—and to impress a very lovely lady. What kind of job did Cassie think he was doing?

"Who is it? Who is it?" Makayla asked, echoing the question going through Wade's mind.

Cassie put the slip of paper on the breakfast bar behind her. "Jack gets to go first."

The little boy ran into the living room and immediately embraced the board covered with the image of one of the latest cartoon characters. Wade smiled, because he'd picked that board with Jack in mind.

"Hey, buddy, that board's almost as big as you are."

"Mr. Wade, will you carry my board to the beach?" Jack asked, his blue eyes filled with anxiety.

"Sure. We'll carry it together."

Then Cassie pulled another slip from the bowl and looked at it. "Taylor, your turn."

Taylor squealed and ran to claim her board. Wade glanced at Cassie, who appeared to be as surprised as he was by Taylor's uncharacteristic display of joy.

"The last one's yours, Makayla." Cassie patted the little girl on the back.

Clapping her hands in excitement, Makayla sprinted into the living room, then jogged in place in front of the pink board with a cute little cartoon girl on it who looked a lot like her. She picked it up and held it out in front of her. "This is the one I wanted." Then she set the board down and ran over to Wade and gave him a big hug. "Thank you, Mr. Wade."

"You're welcome, Makayla," Wade replied, his heart turning to mush. He picked up Jack's board and headed for the door, then stopped. "Oops. Forgot to put on our sunscreen. Let's do that before we go out to the beach."

In a few minutes, everyone was covered in sunscreen and had donned beach hats. Wade showed off his new khaki hat. "No flowers on this one."

"You kinda look like Indiana Jones from one of the early movies in that hat," Cassie said.

"Definitely better than the flowered one," he said, not knowing for sure how he should respond. Wow! She thought he looked like a young Harrison Ford. He'd take that any day, but then reminded himself not to let anything go to his head. Maybe she wasn't thinking of the actor. Then he reminded himself that even a younger Harrison Ford was much older than Cassie.

Making sure to keep his ego in check, Wade helped Jack carry his board and, at the same time, assisted Cassie with the beach cart. "Hauling all this stuff is quite a task. Too bad we can't store it on the beach."

"Nice idea, but not practical. If the wind and waves didn't get it, someone on the beach would consider it abandoned and help themselves."

"You're right."

Heat and humidity blanketed them as they trooped across the walkover with all their paraphernalia and finally reached the beach. Wade set up two beach chairs near the water's edge and hung a towel over each one, while Cassie set up Danny's playpen and tent.

Hoping all the activity would help keep him from thinking too much about Cassie, Wade showed Taylor, Makayla and Jack how to use the straps attached to their bodyboards. "Put this around your wrist so your board doesn't float away from you."

In a few minutes, Cassie joined Wade and the older children near the chairs. "I gave Danny a bunch of balls and toys to play with, so I hope he'll be content in there for a while. At least until we get the kids started on the bodyboards."

"First, I think I'll show them how the boards work. What do you think?"

"Sounds good to me. I want to see this demonstration myself." She gave him an impish grin.

He wondered whether she might think he wasn't very proficient with a bodyboard. She probably thought he was too old to indulge in such activities. Well, he would show her he wasn't old. Just give him a wave to ride....

For a minute, he'd forgotten about the kids. He'd better keep his head on straight and not get distracted by a pretty face—or the need to impress her with a youthful pursuit.

He turned his attention to the kids, who stood in stair-step fashion, much as they'd done the first day he'd seen them. Amazingly enough, they were standing still, staring at him and waiting for instructions, even live-wire Makayla. "Jack, may I use your board?"

"Yes, sir." Nodding vigorously, Jack handed his board to Wade.

"Thanks, little buddy." Wade surveyed the group. "Have any of you ever ridden on a bodyboard?"

"No, sir," they said in unison. They looked at him, wide-eyed with anticipation.

"You wait right here by the edge of the water, and I'll show you how to ride the board."

"Yes, sir." They stood very still, their little feet making imprints in the soft, wet sand.

"Who wants to hold my new hat?"

"I'll hold it," Taylor replied first.

"Here you go. Now take good care of it," Wade said, thinking he definitely didn't want anything to happen to the hat that made him look like Indiana Jones.

Carrying the board at his side, he made his way into the surf. He feared they were expecting him to perform some spectacular feat. And how would Cassie see him if he fell off and made a fool of himself? He hadn't really thought this whole thing through. But he couldn't back out now.

Suddenly he remembered his glasses. Oh, that would've been really cool, to lose his glasses in the ocean. Sheepishly, he turned back. "Forgot to take off my glasses. I'll leave them on the chair."

Turning around, he waved at the kids, even though they looked a little fuzzy without his glasses. "Okay, watch how I catch a wave and ride it to the beach."

Makayla waved back at him. "I'm watching."

He trudged into the surf, where relatively small waves foamed around his legs. The cool water was refreshing after the trek from the town houses. As he pushed his way into deeper water, the cresting waves foamed around his waist. He tasted the salt spray sprinkling his face. When a sudden strong breeze threatened to rip the board from his hand, he gripped it tighter.

Placing the bodyboard on the water's surface, he watched the waves and waited for just the right one. On his first attempt at catching a wave, he was unceremoniously dumped from the board. He came up sputtering, just in time to have an unusually large wave almost knock him off his feet. The board, which was strapped to his wrist, bobbed harmlessly in the surf. Good thing he'd taken off his glasses, or they'd be lying somewhere on the ocean floor. Laughter and applause filled the air.

Makayla clapped and did a little jig on the sand. "Mr. Wade, that was funny. Do it again!"

Laughing at himself, he kept his blurry gaze on the kids. "That's not the way it's supposed to be done. This time will be better."

Wade was too embarrassed to look at Cassie, especially since she'd be out of focus. Thankfully, even if he looked, his bad vision would make it impossible to see her expression. So much for showing her his athletic prowess.

He laid the board on the water again. This time, he watched the movement of the water as he waited for just the right wave that would crest in the perfect place. When a swell grew taller and closer, he held the edges of the board and hopped on. Paddling madly, he positioned himself as the wave crashed forward. The water grabbed the board and lifted him above the frothing foam of the breaker, holding him suspended while the bubbling water propelled him toward the sand. While the board raced across the surface of the water, he held on tightly until he came skimming onto the beach, right at the children's feet.

Squealing with delight, the kids jumped up and down and clapped their hands. They gathered around him as he jumped to his feet and picked up the board, which was still strapped to his arm. He grabbed a towel from the nearby chair and wiped his face, then grabbed his glasses and put them on. Good. Now he could see what was happening, instead of guessing. Slinging the towel back over the chair, he retrieved his hat from Taylor and put it on. "Who wants to give it a try?"

"Me, me, me!" they cried, all clamoring for his attention.

Stupid, stupid question. Of course they all wanted to give it a try. How patient would they be while they had to take turns getting instructions? There was no way he could just turn them loose on their own, even though Cassie and he would both be nearby. How did Cassie manage to do the right thing with the kids, when he was constantly making the wrong decision?

He glanced her way, and she smiled wryly, as if she could read his thoughts. She knew he was in trouble, but she had no idea that his biggest problem was keeping her off his mind. Thankfully, the kids were there to prevent him from doing something he would regret, such as taking her in his arms and kissing that smile off her lips.

Smiling wider, she sauntered over. "Would you like some help?"

"I thought you'd never ask."

"Aunt Cassie, I want to see you ride the bodyboard," Makayla said, tugging on Cassie's aqua cover-up.

"Yeah, I think Aunt Cassie should show us how it's done, right, kids?" Wade turned and grinned back at her.

"Aunt Cassie, Aunt Cassie, Aunt Cassie!" the kids chanted, clapping their hands.

Sighing, Cassie took off her cover-up and laid it on one of the beach chairs. He forced himself not to stare; she was a beautiful young woman. But more important than her outward beauty was her beautiful spirit. He removed his glasses and pinched the bridge of his nose. He needed to keep his mind on her spirit. He popped his glasses back on just as she took the bodyboard that Makayla shoved at her.

Strapping the cord on her wrist, she eyed Wade and gave him another wry smile. "I won't forget this. You'd better watch out for a little payback."

Wade chuckled as she walked into the surf. "Have fun. I'll be watching."

Glancing back at him, she gave him a mock-venomous look. "Don't worry. I intend to have lots of fun this afternoon."

Something told Wade he might just be the brunt of

that fun, but despite her threat, he was enjoying the interaction. She made him feel alive, refreshed, young, at least when she wasn't calling him sir. Maybe he was enjoying it a little too much.

While Wade and the kids watched, Cassie showed them in one swift lesson how to ride a bodyboard. Without the slightest problem, she rode the perfect wave right onto the beach, hopped up and handed the board to Makayla.

"You did good, Aunt Cassie, better than Mr. Wade. He fell off." Makayla fumbled to put the strap back around her wrist.

Cassie reached down to help the little girl. "Thanks. Now it's your turn."

While Cassie took a moment to wipe her face with a blue and white beach towel, Makayla dashed into the water and tried to hop onto the bodyboard, but the board darted out from under her. The strap kept it from floating away, and she was able to reel it back in. She tried again, but still didn't succeed.

"I can't do this!" she wailed as she came out of the water and plopped down on the sand with the board sitting on her lap.

Wade hunkered down beside her. "Yes, you can. Your aunt Cassie and I will help you get started."

"I don't think I want to do it." Taylor dropped her board to the sand and sat on it. "It looks too scary."

Cassie sat down beside Taylor. "That's up to you, sweetie. If you just want to watch, that's fine."

"I'm not scared. I wanna ride my board," Jack announced as he headed toward the water, dragging his bodyboard behind him.

"Wait a minute." Wade jumped up and waylaid Jack before he reached the water. "You can't go into the ocean until either your aunt Cassie or I go with you."

"But Makayla did."

Wade looked down at Jack. "And look what happened to her."

Before he could say anything else, a loud noise came from inside the little tent. Danny was banging a little plastic shovel against the side of the playpen. "Out! Out!"

"Sounds like Danny's not happy in the playpen anymore." Wade stood behind Jack and placed his hands on Jack's shoulders just to make sure the child didn't get any ideas about going into the ocean by himself. "What do you want to do?"

"I'll get him." Cassie hopped up and went over to the little tent. She plucked Danny from the playpen and set him on the ground. He toddled over to where Taylor sat on her bodyboard. He sat on the board with Taylor and started digging in the sand with his shovel. He seemed content.

"Taylor, since you don't want to do the bodyboard, will you watch Danny while Mr. Wade and I help Makayla and Jack?"

"Yes, ma'am."

"Thank you. Please don't let him go into the water, okay?"

Taylor nodded. "I'll get a pail and another shovel, and we'll dig in the sand.

"Okay." Cassie walked over and held out her hand to Makayla. "You ready to try again?"

"Yes, ma'am." Makayla grabbed Cassie's hand.

"Let's go." Cassie pulled the child to her feet, then glanced over at Wade and smiled.

That smile made him think of all kinds of things he shouldn't be thinking. He wanted to pull her close and hold her in his arms. He wished there weren't four little kids with them. But entertaining romantic notions about her was only going to lead to trouble. How many times had he told himself that? Yet his thoughts always came back to that very idea.

Jack tapped him on the arm. "Mr. Wade, are we going to go in the water?"

"Yeah," Wade replied, shaking himself from his wayward thoughts. "Come on."

After placing his glasses and hat on the beach chair, Wade followed Cassie and Makayla into the surf. Jack charged after them but stopped short when a wave nearly knocked him off his feet.

"Whoa there, little buddy. You'd better let me give you a hand." Wade picked Jack up and carried him while the bodyboard floated behind them.

Wade glanced over at Cassie. She already had Makayla lying facedown on her bodyboard while she bobbed up and down on the incoming waves. When Wade and Cassie were about waist deep in the surf, Wade set Jack on his board and pointed to Makayla. "You see how she's lying on her stomach?" The little boy nodded. "I want you to do the same thing. I'll hold your board right here while you do that."

"Yes, sir." Jack shifted around until he was lying facedown.

"Put your hands right up here." Wade placed Jack's hands on each side of the board. "Now hold on tight."

"I'm ready. I'm holdin' on." The little boy's knuckles were white as he gripped the board.

"Okay, here we go." Pushing the bodyboard ahead, Wade moved slowly through the water. He watched carefully for a good wave. As one formed a few yards away from them, he moved the board into place. As the wave began to crest, he waited for just the right moment. Then he shoved the board ahead to catch the foaming water of the breaker. Letting go of the board, he yelled, "Hang on!"

The wave picked up the bodyboard and carried Jack through the surf. Wade chased after it while Jack squealed with delight.

Jack and the bodyboard glided to a stop on the sand. The little boy scrambled to his feet and turned around, all smiles. "That was fun. I wanna go again."

Laughing, Wade scooped Jack into his arms. "Okay, little buddy, but first let's see how your sister and aunt are doing."

Wade scanned the area with his fuzzy vision until he spotted Cassie. She stood waist-deep in the water with Makayla clinging to her neck. Why wasn't Makayla riding her bodyboard? She'd been so excited about it. He carried Jack into the water as his board bounced in the surf behind them.

When Wade reached Cassie's side, he could see that Makayla had been crying. "What's wrong?"

Shrugging, Cassie shook her head. "She suddenly got very frightened for some reason, and she won't tell me why."

"Makayla, how come you don't want to ride your bodyboard?"

Without answering, Makayla buried her head on Cassie's shoulder, her legs wrapped around Cassie's waist.

"Will you come see me?" Wade asked.

"I don't want to get in the water," Makayla mumbled, barely lifting her head.

"You won't have to get in the water. I'll hold you up."

"Promise?"

"Promise." Wade looked down at Jack. "Do you want to go to your aunt Cassie or lie on your board?"

"Can Aunt Cassie help me ride?" Jack asked.

Wade glanced at Cassie. "You want to trade kids?"

"Sure."

Wade helped Jack lie on his stomach on his body-board. When the little boy was settled and had a firm grip on the board, he pushed it in the water until Cassie was able to grip it with her free hand. Then he reached out to take Makayla from Cassie. Their hands brushed as they made the exchange, and Wade forced himself not to think about how Cassie's slightest touch affected him. He needed to keep his mind on helping Makayla.

The little girl clung to him, and he could feel her trembling. What could have scared her so much? He turned to Cassie and said, "I'm going to take her out of the water. We'll go sit on the beach with Taylor and Danny. Maybe I can find out why she's so afraid."

"Okay, I'll see if I can manage to give Jack as good a ride as you did." Cassie held Jack and his bodyboard in one spot as it bobbed up and down on the waves.

Wade carried Makayla and her bodyboard back to the beach. He set her down next to Taylor and Danny, who had dug a big hole in the sand. Without a word, Makayla grabbed a plastic shovel and started to help them. Wade quickly went to his chair to get his glasses and hat.

After he put them on, he looked toward the ocean. Cassie had just let go of Jack and his board. He was riding a wave, his delighted squeal piercing the air. Cassie jogged after him, and Wade couldn't help watching her. Her dark, wet curls swayed around her shoulders as she chased Jack through the water. She laughed at Jack's joy. When he skidded to a stop in the sand, she scooped him up into her arms. He giggled, and she gave him a big, noisy kiss on the cheek. He laughed some more. Then they headed back into the water for another ride.

Wade's heart was racing as fast as the bodyboard skimming the water. With visions of her kissing *him* on the cheek planted in his mind, he forced himself to look away. He shook his head to rid himself of the image. Wishing wasn't going to make it happen. *Could* he make it happen? He didn't want to answer that question, so he forced himself to think about Makayla.

Sinking down on the sand beside the little girl, he just sat there for a moment and helped her dig, hoping she would give him some clue about her fear. When she remained quiet, he finally asked, "Can you tell me why you didn't want to ride your bodyboard?"

"I'm afraid of the sharks."

"There aren't any sharks out there."

"But I saw them."

"Why didn't you tell your aunt Cassie?"

"I just wanted to get out of the water," she said, as if her fear had made her forget that everyone would be in trouble if there really were sharks in the water.

"Are you sure you saw sharks?"

Makayla nodded very slowly. "Yes, sir. I saw their fins."

"Where?"

Makayla pointed straight ahead at the ocean. "Out there."

"I saw them, too," Taylor chimed in. "Right out there where Makayla said."

Wade stared at the two little girls. Sharks? Were there really sharks in this area? He hadn't even considered it when they had ventured into the water. He'd better tell Cassie and try not to scare Jack.

Standing, he scanned the water for any sign of fins of any sort. No fins, but a number of people were jumping waves, riding waves on bodyboards or surfing the shallow water on skimboards. A few yards down the beach, a couple of fishermen, sitting lazily in lawn chairs, had their lines in the water. Did the bait attract sharks, as well as other fish?

Wade met Cassie and Jack as the little boy ended another ride nearby. Wade motioned for them to come near. "Cassie, I think I've figured out why Makayla's afraid."

"Why?"

Wade glanced down at Jack. "Hey, buddy, why don't you go play with your sisters for a minute, and then we'll see about some more rides on your bodyboard, okay?"

"Yes, sir." Leaving his bodyboard at Wade's feet, Jack raced across the sand to join Makayla and Taylor.

"So what did you find out?" Cassie dried off with the towel she'd grabbed from the beach chair.

Wade turned his back to the children as he looked at Cassie. "Have you ever heard of shark attacks on this beach?"

Her eyebrows rose. "Shark attacks? Not recently. Not any bad ones that I can remember."

"Well, Makayla and Taylor said they saw fins."

Cassie's nose wrinkled, and her eyebrows scrunched up in a frown. "They did?"

Wade nodded. "What do you think?"

"I don't know what to think." Sighing loudly, she turned to look at the ocean. "Maybe we ought to sit out for a while and just kind of watch the area before we do any more bodyboarding."

"Sounds good to me." Wade glanced over his shoulder at the kids. "Do you think Jack will protest?"

"Just let him keep playing there, and if he asks, we'll just say we're taking a rest."

"Good idea." Wade couldn't help thinking how wise Cassie was in dealing with these kids. If only he could be as wise in dealing with her and the way his feelings for her had grown.

Wade made himself comfortable in his beach chair and tried not to keep glancing at Cassie as she reapplied her sunscreen. "Should we all do that?"

"Yeah, if we don't want to have sunburns. And that'll also give us a good reason not to go back in the water." Cassie called the kids over, and soon everyone was slathering sunscreen on every inch of exposed skin. "Okay, everyone, we're going to stay out of the water for a while, so we won't wash off the sunscreen."

"Yes, ma'am," the children replied, and immediately went back to digging their hole.

Cassie and Wade settled in their chairs again. After donning his hat and glasses, Wade got out a book, but his attention was focused on the ocean. He kept watching the other people having a good time in the surf without a care and hoped the little girls had been wrong about what they'd seen. Surely if there were sharks, he would have seen them also.

Then in the distance, he saw fins as arched backs came out of the water in tandem. A few yards away they appeared again. Dolphins. Is that what the girls had seen? He jumped up from his chair, and without turning around, he called, "Makayla, Taylor, come here."

The little girls came immediately to his side. "Yes, sir, what do you want?"

He pointed toward the area where he'd last seen the dolphins surface. "Watch right out there."

Makayla's eyes grew wide. "Did you see the sharks?"

"Not sharks. Dolphins. Keep watching."

While they stood with their gazes trained on the water, Cassie picked up Danny and ushered Jack over to join them in their vigil. "So you saw dolphins? That's a relief."

Looking out at the ocean, Makayla squinted. "I don't see anything."

Taylor pulled on Wade's arm and pointed to the right. "I see them."

Wade looked in that direction. "Yeah, those are dolphins." Then he turned to Taylor and Makayla. "Girls, is that what you saw?"

The girls nodded. "Yes, sir."

While Cassie pointed the dolphins out to Jack, Wade hunkered down beside the girls. "You don't have to be afraid of dolphins. They won't hurt us."

The graceful animals continued to appear and disappear at regular intervals. Cassie seemed as much in awe of the spectacle as the kids. Wade stood and let his gaze linger on her. The breeze blew a damp curl across her check, and he longed to reach out and push it aside.

Instead, he gripped the back of his beach chair. His heart was leaping like the dolphins. Keeping his feelings in check got more difficult every time they were together.

The argument for not letting his feelings for her show seemed to have been lost. Selfish or not—he wasn't going to run away from finding out what might happen between them.

Chapter Ten

Cassie glanced at Wade, who was standing there gripping the back of his beach chair. Letting out a little sigh, she bounced Danny in her arms. Every time she looked at Wade in that Indiana Jones hat, a warm sensation curled around her heart. He wasn't just kind to the kids. He was everything she had ever dreamed of in a man.

Dreams. Could they come true?

Sometimes she thought he looked at her like he was going to pat her on the head, the same way he did Taylor and Makayla. How could she show him she wasn't just one of the kids?

He turned and looked at her with a smile. "So what do you think? Now that we've solved the mystery of the fins, should we do a little more bodyboarding or pack it up and go in?"

"Let's see what the kids want to do," she said, trying to ignore the way her stomach did a little flip-flop like one of the dolphins jumping in and out of the water. She really didn't want to go, because leaving would probably mean the end of her time with Wade, but she needed to put the kids' interests before her own.

"Good idea." He turned back to the children, who had resumed their digging. "Does anyone want to ride body-boards again?"

Immediately Jack jumped up and poked his finger on his chest. "Me. I not afraid of fins."

Wade pressed his lips together, and Cassie was sure he was fighting back a little laughter. "What about you girls?"

"I'm going to dig," Taylor said, shaking her head.

Makayla held up her shovel. "Me, too."

Wade removed his hat and glasses while Jack picked up his board and tried to put the strap on his wrist. Wade hunkered down to help him. "Looks like it's you and me, bud. Let's head for the surf."

The little boy grabbed Wade's hand, and they walked into the water. Cassie's heart zinged; she felt as though it were beating outside her chest. The sight of Wade and Jack made her wish—wish that Wade could be the kids' daddy. No, she shouldn't go there. That was wishing for too much too soon. She had to quit thinking like Makayla.

Soon Wade had Jack riding the waves. Cassie sat in her beach chair and took in their fun. Every time Jack came to a stop on the beach, he hopped up and begged to go again. He was going to wear Wade out.

Despite Jack's bravado, maybe he needed to be a lit-tle more cautious about what might be lurking in the ocean. She didn't want to teach him fear, just a healthy respect for the dangers that might be there. She could talk to Wade about how to deal with the subject later. It was nice to have a sounding board living next door—a good-looking sounding board.

She gave herself a mental shake. She was at it again—thinking stuff about Wade that was better left alone. She should think of him as a mentor, the same as Angie. Since Angie wasn't as close by as she'd been when Cassie lived in Jacksonville, God had sent Wade. He was someone older and wiser, who could give her advice. That was the way she'd looked at him when they first met, and she needed to keep seeing him in that light.

Last Sunday's sermon, about Barnabas, came to mind. Barnabas had been a good man, an encourager, who helped people remain true to the Lord. Wade was a modern-day Barnabas, sent to encourage her in life and in her walk with the Lord. God knew how to put people in place to help others. So why did all this romance stuff have to keep creeping into her mind?

While Cassie stood there lost in her thoughts about Wade, she felt a little tap on one arm. She glanced down.

Holding her bodyboard, Makayla looked up at her. "I wanna bodyboard."

"You do?"

"Yes, ma'am."

Cassie turned to check on Taylor. "How about you, Taylor?"

Barely meeting Cassie's gaze, the little girl nodded, a tiny smile curving her lips. "Yes, ma'am."

"Okay. Get your bodyboards ready." Cassie set Danny down.

He waddled over to Makayla and grabbed hold of her board. She tried to jerk it away from him. "Danny, stop it. You're too little to bodyboard."

When she pulled it from his grip, he plopped down on the sand and began to cry. Cassie raced over and picked him up. Bouncing him in her arms, she stared down at Makayla. "You can't be shoving him around. He's just a baby."

Makayla frowned. "Well, he was trying to take my board."

"If you're going to fuss, you won't get to go at all."

"What's happening here?"

Cassie turned at the sound of Wade's voice. He stood there, his tanned skin dripping with water. For a moment, she forgot to breathe. He was beginning to resemble one of those surfer dudes in the movies. Several weeks of fun in the sun had changed his appearance dramatically. But she shouldn't even be thinking about how good he looked. She was having a lot of trouble with that recently, especially today. She needed to get her mind focused on Wade's question, not on his appearance.

"Um…oh, Makayla and Danny were having a tug-of-war with her bodyboard, and Danny lost." Cassie motioned toward Taylor, then Makayla. "The girls would like to give bodyboarding a try after all."

"Jack and I are going to take a little break. I'll watch Jack and Danny, if you want to help the girls ride their boards."

Cassie glanced at Taylor. "You want to go first?"

"Yes, ma'am."

With her board dragging behind her, Makayla planted herself in front of Cassie. "Why can't I go first?"

"Because you already had a chance. Taylor will go, then you. You can help Mr. Wade watch Danny and Jack."

"That's boring," Makayla said, sticking out her bottom lip.

"If you're going to pout, you won't get to go."

"I'll help. I'll help." Makayla scurried over to play with Jack, who had resumed digging the hole, which had grown big enough to accommodate one of the kids.

While Wade kept an eye on Makayla and the boys, Cassie took Taylor into the water and showed her how to hold on to her bodyboard. On Taylor's first ride, the look on her face was a mixture of joy and fear. But when she came to a skidding halt on the sand, she jumped up and asked to go again.

Seeing Taylor's reaction was priceless. The shy little girl was having the time of her life. After she took a couple more rides, Cassie gave Makayla a turn. Cassie was sure Makayla's screams of delight as she rode the waves could be heard at the Ritz. Despite all the times Makayla aggravated Cassie with her behavior, she savored these moments. Makayla's life was so much better now than before. All the children had better lives thanks to God and Angie. Now Wade was part of that picture, too.

What would it be like to have him as a permanent part of the picture? The question stopped her in her tracks while she waited for Makayla to bring her board into the water again. Waves swirled around her legs as her gaze wandered to the beach, where Wade was helping the kids dig their hole. Her heart fluttered at the sight.

Ever since she'd met him, his attention to the children had touched her, had created a longing in her heart—a longing so deep it produced improbable scenarios in her mind. While she stood there dreaming, a big wave jarred her off her feet and knocked her mind back to reality. Her thoughts were impractical, impetuous, impossible. Pushing them away, she helped Makayla position her board for another ride.

When Makayla's bodyboard reached the beach, Jack wandered into the surf and begged Cassie to let him ride again. After Cassie discussed the situation with Wade, they decided the kids would take turns getting rides and the adults would take turns watching Danny. Soon they were all playing together in the water.

Finally, the older children tired of riding the bodyboards. After everyone reapplied sunscreen and put on their beach hats, the older children went back to digging their hole. Cassie put Danny in his playpen under the little tent, and he fell asleep almost immediately. Wade had set up the beach umbrella over the chairs, and he was reading his book when Cassie plopped onto the chair beside him.

She let out a long, slow breath. "Danny's out for the count, but the other three are still going strong. They wore me out. What about you?"

"Yeah. It feels good to sit down."

"We've been out here for a couple of hours. I hope we won't all look like lobsters tomorrow."

"That's why I put up the umbrella."

"I think if I closed my eyes, I might nod off like Danny."

"Well, don't do that. One of us needs to stay awake to keep an eye on the kids."

Cassie laughed. "Are you telling me you're going to take a nap?"

Wade nodded. "I just might. I'm going to give this book a try, but I can't make any promises I'll stay awake."

"So no nap for me?"

He chuckled. "Seems that way. Besides, you don't need a nap. You're the younger one."

"How young do you think I am?" she asked, deciding this might be a good time to actually find out their age difference—not that it had any bearing on anything. She should pound that thought home.

Taking the clips off his glasses, he studied her for a moment. While he scrutinized her, her insides churned like the nearby breakers. Was he thinking she was just a kid? Probably.

He popped the clips back on and settled down in his chair. "Twenty-one."

"Angie told you, didn't she?"

A crooked grin crept across his face. "No, but I guessed right, huh?"

"You did. How?"

"I'm a good guesser. Now it's your turn."

"To guess your age?"

"Yeah." His grin grew wider.

Glancing at the kids, Cassie almost wished one of them would start a fuss and rescue her from having to guess Wade's age. What if she said he was older than he really was? He'd be insulted. But she was sure he was a least a dozen years older. So she should just spit out her answer. Why was she worrying? This whole age thing was nonsense. She took a deep breath and let it out in a big whoosh. "Thirty-three."

"Close."

"How close?"

"One year."

Cassie breathed a mental sigh of relief. "Lower or higher?"

"Don't you still have to guess?"

Smiling, she shook her head. "I'll just think of you as thirty-three. One year one way or the other isn't going to make any difference."

He laughed halfheartedly. "Yeah, I suppose you're right. To someone who's twenty-one, thirty-something probably seems pretty old. When I was your age, I remember thinking anyone over thirty was over-the-hill."

"Oh, I don't think you're over-the-hill. Angie thinks she's over-the-hill because she's over fifty, but I don't even think she's that old."

"I think you're protesting too much," he said with a chuckle. "I bet the first time you saw me, you—"

"I thought you were somewhere in your early-thirties."

"Yeah, and that seemed old to you, right?"

He had her there, but she didn't feel that way anymore, not now that she knew him. She didn't want to lie, and she didn't want to let him know she had thought of him as old. Maybe, like he said, those were just the natural thoughts of someone her age. There was no getting around it. He thought she was a kid. Nothing was going to change that.

"Your silence says it all." He raised his eyebrows in a got-you-now expression.

"Not old, just older than me."

"Same thing." He reached over and patted her hand. "It's okay. I thought you probably felt that way." He laid his head back on his chair. "This old man is going to take a nap."

Trying to remember that the touch of his hand was only a meaningless gesture, Cassie decided not to protest his calling himself old. It would only prolong the futile discussion and remind him that she was so much younger. Maybe that was all right. If she and the kids included him in all their activities, he might not see himself as older and her as younger and age wouldn't make a difference. *Yeah, right.*

While Wade lounged in his chair, Cassie hopped up and went to check on Danny. She poked her head inside the little tent and found him still sleeping. She glanced at the other kids. With his beach hat on his head, Jack was sitting in the big hole, and the girls were covering him with the sand. He appeared to be enjoying every minute as more and more of his body disappeared under a pile of sand.

She moseyed over to their project. When she stopped in front of the mound of sand, covering Jack, he grinned up at her. "Aunt Cassie, I'm gettin' buried."

"Whose idea was this?"

"Mine." Makayla raised her hand. "Do you want to get buried?"

"No, it doesn't look like fun to me."

"It's fun to put the sand on." Taylor dumped another shovelful on the pile and patted it down.

"Do you think Mr. Wade would let us bury him?" Makayla asked.

Cassie glanced over her shoulder. "I don't know. He's resting. Maybe he'd like to rest in your pit when you're finished with Jack, but you'll need a bigger hole for Mr. Wade."

"We can dig a really big hole for him." Makayla immediately started making a new hole next to Jack.

"Okay, you let me know when you've got it ready."

Cassie returned to her chair and glanced at Wade. Was he asleep? She couldn't tell, with his hat pulled down so it covered his eyes. She couldn't even see his glasses with the sun clips on them. His head lolled off to one side, and his book lay closed on his lap. She carefully removed the book. He didn't twitch a muscle. He had to be sleeping. This was the perfect chance to get him back for the bodyboard incident.

After checking on Danny one more time, she hurried to the beach cart. She dug down in the center compartment and pulled out a large water launcher that she'd seen the first time she packed the cart. She hadn't shown it to the kids because there was only one, and she didn't want them fighting over it. But this was the perfect way to get the payback she'd promised Wade.

The kids were still engrossed in burying Jack and digging their hole for Wade and weren't paying a bit of attention to her. She went quietly down to the water's edge and filled the chamber of the launcher with water. After priming the pump, she pressed the trigger. A stream of water shot out thirty feet into the waves. It worked.

Turning, she glanced at Wade. Did she dare? He was such a prime target. She let the launcher fall to her side. Was this any way to make the man think she wasn't one of the kids? Absolutely not, but then, the age thing was never going to go away, and this was too tempting. Wouldn't squirting him with water count toward treating *him* as one of the kids and making him feel younger? *That* was the way she would look at it.

She stood there for a while, watching him sleep. Her finger moved back and forth on the trigger. Should she do this? Did she know him well enough? Surely he was just the kind of guy who would take it all in fun.

She would start off slowly, with a little stream of water. Standing in the surf several feet away, she aimed at his feet and pulled the trigger. When the water hit his feet, he jerked but didn't appear to wake up. She aimed higher at his legs. There was still no major reaction when the water hit them. Finally, she aimed for his chest and pulled the trigger.

As soon as the water hit Wade's chest, he was out of his chair. Grinning, he charged into the surf after her. "So is this the payback you warned me about?"

"Yes. You deserved it." She raced away through the surf, her feet kicking up a spray of water as she went.

"That's a matter of opinion," he yelled, chasing her through the water.

"Think of how many times I've fed you," she called, trying to outrace him. "Remember that old saying, 'Don't bite the hand that feeds you.'"

"I'm not going to bite you." He laughed and continued to close the gap between them. "I'm only going to squirt you with water when I take that thing away from you."

Cassie ran out of the ocean and onto the beach, her feet sinking into the wet sand as she tried without success to outrun him. When he caught her, he took hold of one of her arms and pulled her to a stop. She tried to get out of his grasp. When she turned, he was grinning at her.

"I've got you now. I'll take the water launcher."

Standing on her tiptoes, she held it as high as she could. "Oh, no, you won't."

"Oh, yes, I will." He reached up and tried to wrestle the launcher from her hand.

When he let go of her other arm in an effort to seize the launcher, she used both hands to hold it tighter. Because he was taller, he had very little trouble reaching over her head and grabbing the launcher. As he pulled on it, he stepped nearer. Her heart began to hammer, and all she could think of was how close he was standing.

She lost her grip on the launcher, and he wrenched it from her hands.

"Now it's your turn to get wet." He stepped back, a mischievous smile curving his mouth.

Trying to catch her breath, she squealed as he started squirting her. She ran, hoping to get away from the stream of water, but she still couldn't outrun him. Finally, she picked up one of the bodyboards and used it as a shield. The water made a thudding sound as it hit the board and sprayed away. She managed to deflect some of the squirts, but she couldn't move the board fast enough. She danced around, attempting to outmaneuver him, but to no avail. He continued squirting her until she doubled over with laughter and more squeals.

"I give…I give…" she pleaded between bursts of laughter.

Suddenly, Jack appeared, covered from head to toe with sand, and started beating on Wade's legs. "Don't hurt Aunt Cassie!"

Cassie and Wade stopped and looked at each other. Her heart sank into her stomach. The little boy had completely misunderstood their playful battle.

Wade dropped the launcher and hunkered down next to Jack, who continued to pommel him. "Hey, little buddy, it's all right. Your aunt Cassie and I were just playing a game."

Quickly kneeling next to Jack, Cassie took hold of his arms so he couldn't pound his tiny fists on Wade. "Jack, sweetie, please don't hit Mr. Wade. He's not trying to hurt me. We were just playing."

She hugged the little boy to her, not caring that she was now also covered with sand. He hugged her back and wouldn't let go. Finally, she picked him up. His little arms clung to her neck.

Wade stood with them. He looked at her and mouthed the words, "I'm sorry. What should we do?"

"Don't worry. We'll talk to him," she mouthed back.

"Jack, will you talk to me?" Wade asked.

Shaking his head, the little boy buried his face on Cassie's shoulder. As she held him, Taylor and Makayla joined the group. Cassie looked down at them. "Do you girls understand that Mr. Wade and I were just playing a game?"

The girls nodded. "Yes, ma'am."

"Can I shoot the water?" Makayla looked over at Wade, who still held the launcher.

Cassie tried to set Jack down, but he clung tighter. Then Danny started to cry. Sighing, she glanced from the tent to Wade. "Would you show the girls how to use the launcher?"

Wade nodded. "Come on, girls. Let's go fill this thing with water.

Watching Taylor and Makayla scamper after Wade as he went toward the surf made her heart ache. She gave their little brother a squeeze. "Jack, I need to check on Danny. Will you help me?"

Jack lifted his head. Tears stained his reddened cheeks. "What's Mr. Wade going to do to me?"

"He's not going to do anything to you."

"That's what Mama used to say, but then Daddy would lock us in the room."

"Oh, sugar, that's not going to happen here."

"Promise?"

"Promise."

Jack squirmed to get down. Relieved, Cassie set him on the ground. He was still covered with sand from head to toe. The sight of his sandy little body made her want to laugh, but the remnants of his tears brought a sad pressure to her heart. The warring emotions made her press her lips together as she fought back laughter and tears.

Taking Jack's hand, Cassie led him over to the tent. Danny held out his little arms, begging to be picked up. She started to reach out for him, but looked down at herself. She was covered with sand. If she picked him up, the sand would rub off on him, too. She didn't want everyone to be a sandy mess. Could she possibly pick him up without passing the sand on to him? She rubbed her hands together until they felt sand-free. Lifting him, she held him away from her body and set him down. He toddled away toward the ocean, where Wade and the girls were filling the launcher. Jack clung to her leg, so she couldn't chase after Danny.

"Taylor, grab Danny before he gets into the water!" Cassie yelled.

"Yes, ma'am," Taylor replied and managed to nab Danny a second before he reached the surf.

"Good job." Cassie gave Taylor the thumbs-up sign, then looked down at Jack. "You and I need to get this sand off ourselves. "You want to go into the water and wash it off?"

When he nodded, Cassie picked him up and carried him into the ocean, where the waves bubbled around her legs. She walked chest-deep into the water. Then she bobbed up and down, letting the waves wash away the sand. While they dipped into the water, she kept an eye on Taylor, Danny, Makayla and Wade.

The waves sloshed around her and swayed her back and forth. Feeling that most of the sand had been washed away, she moved closer to the shore, where Wade was instructing Taylor and Makayla on how to use the launcher. He gave it to Taylor and stood back. She pressed the trigger. A stream of water spewed from the launcher and soaked Wade. Taylor giggled with glee.

Jumping up and down, Makayla clapped her hands. "I want to squirt him next. My turn. My turn."

Cassie chuckled when Danny started jumping up and down and clapping his hands, too. While Danny did an imitation of Makayla's clapping and jumping, Taylor handed the launcher to her sister. She immediately started squirting Wade. He tried to dodge the stream of water, but with little success—much to her delight. Danny and Taylor continued the applause and laughter.

Squirming in Cassie's arms, Jack pointed at Wade and the girls. "I wanna do that."

"Are you sure?"

"Yes, ma'am."

Cassie set Jack on the ground. "If you want to use the launcher, you'll have to talk to Mr. Wade."

With his lips pressed together and his shoulders humped up to his ears, Jack looked up at Cassie. He didn't say a word, but Cassie could tell the little boy was, at the same time, fearful and eager. She gave him a tiny push. "Mr. Wade will be glad to help you. Go ask him."

Almost dragging his feet, Jack walked toward the group, his head down. Cassie recognized his trepidation. She wanted to gather him in her arms and keep him from worrying, but he needed to learn that Wade Dalton was not a man like his father. Jack needed a good male role model, and Cassie saw that in Wade. She saw so much to like in Wade that she couldn't deny her growing feelings for him. Were those feelings hopeless? She was afraid to explore them further, because she might discover that they were fruitless.

Before Jack joined Wade and the girls, Cassie caught Wade's attention and pointed down, toward the little boy, and mouthed, "He wants to try it."

Smiling, Wade nodded and gave her the A-OK sign. Then he focused his attention on Jack's approach. Makayla gave the launcher to Wade, and he held it by his side while he waited for Jack. With his head still lowered, Jack stopped in front of Wade.

Cassie remained at a distance and watched the interaction between the man and the little boy. She breathed a sigh of relief when Jack's shoulders relaxed and he looked up. Wade patted Jack on the head and showed him the launcher. Then Wade waved for the children to follow him into the surf. As Danny toddled after them, Cassie intercepted him and carried him to where Wade was showing Jack how to fill the launcher with water.

Soon everyone was taking a turn with the toy as they ran after each other around the beach. Laughter and shouts accompanied the merry chase. Eventually, however, everyone grew tired of the game. After Cassie put the launcher back into the beach cart, she plopped down on the beach chair next to the one Wade occupied. The children continued playing as they took turns getting buried in the sand.

Cassie gazed out at the waves that gently lapped the

beach and said, "Thanks for helping with the kids this afternoon. Sometimes I feel like we're taking advantage of you."

"You're not. I'm here because I enjoy being with you and the kids."

"I'm glad," she said, wondering whether he would enjoy this time if the kids weren't in the picture.

Before she could say anything else, Makayla raced up to her chair. "Aunt Cassie, it's your turn to get buried. We dug a great big hole for you."

Cassie laughed. "But what if I don't want to get buried?"

"Then Mr. Wade can have a turn."

"I think that's a good idea. Let Mr. Wade have his turn." Oh, no. What had she just done? She had put him on the spot to do something he probably didn't want to do. Grimacing, she cast a glance in his direction.

He gave her a lopsided grin. "We should *all* take a turn."

"Okay, but you need to dig another hole, so you can bury us both at the same time," Cassie said, knowing her participation was the least she could do, since she'd volunteered Wade.

"We'll dig a hole for both of you." Makayla scampered away.

Cassie watched the kids spring into action with their little shovels. "I wonder how long that'll take."

Wade chuckled. "Probably not as long as we'd like."

"You're right." Cassie settled back in her beach chair with a sigh. "I'm so sorry about the way Jack acted."

"He didn't hurt me, but I worry that he thought *I* was hurting *you*."

"Well, you seem to have won him over. It was my fault. I started it by using the launcher on you."

"There was no way you could've known Jack's reaction."

"I suppose."

"Are we still on for church and a picnic lunch tomorrow?"

Cassie nodded. "I'm just not sure when to tell the kids about lunch."

"After church?"

"Probably." Cassie turned to check on them. They were still digging holes. Even Danny was helping. As she started to turn around, she noticed the black cloud on the western horizon. She looked back at Wade. "Check out the sky behind us. I think we'd better pack up and head home."

"Looks like rain."

Cassie jumped up from her chair and folded it. "I just hope it's not a repeat of the other night."

"The lifeguards aren't chasing everyone off the beach, so maybe this won't be more than a rain shower." Wade got up and folded his chair and the beach umbrella.

"I hope you're right, because I don't want to get soaked again." Cassie started putting things in the beach cart and told the kids to gather their pails and shovels.

"But we aren't finished digging, and we didn't get to bury you in the sand," Makayla protested.

"You don't have a choice. We need to go in. You can bury us some other day." Cassie hoped Wade didn't mind that she'd volunteered him again.

"Okay." Makayla scowled as she picked up the buckets and shovels.

In a few minutes, they had their gear packed and were heading home. Using the shower at the other end of the walkover, they washed the sand from their bodies, toys and chairs. Then they hurried across the lawn. Just before they reached the patio outside Cassie's town house, the rain started.

Cassie unlocked the patio door. "Okay, kids. Hurry and dry off before you go inside."

"Looks as though we came up from the beach just in time," Wade said, helping Danny and Jack with their towels. Then Wade grabbed his own beach towel and slung it around his neck. "I'll see you tomorrow morning for church."

Makayla jumped in front of him. "Mr. Wade, aren't you going to eat with us tonight?"

Wade glanced down at the little girl. "Thank you for the invitation, Makayla, but I have a dinner engagement tonight. So I have to get ready."

"What does 'dinner 'gagement' mean?"

"It means I'm eating out with someone. And the word is *en…gage…ment,*" Wade replied.

"Oh." Makayla narrowed her gaze as she looked at Wade. "Will you have a dinner *en…gage…ment* with us sometime?"

Nodding, Wade chuckled. "I think that's an excellent idea. I've eaten here enough times. So it should be my treat." Then he glanced at Cassie. "What do you think?"

"You really shouldn't feel obligated. You've helped us more than we've helped you," Cassie said, wondering what kind of dinner engagement Wade had.

"I don't feel obligated. I just want to do it."

"We'll talk about it." Cassie ushered the kids inside

with instructions to change, then turned to Wade. "Tomorrow's picnic should be enough."

"We'll see," Wade called over his shoulder as he dashed toward his town house. He waved as he disappeared behind the wall separating their patios.

While the gentle rain fell, Cassie stood on the patio for a couple of minutes and wondered about Wade and his dinner engagement. Was it some kind of date? She had to admit she hoped it wasn't. Jealousy was knocking on the door to her heart, but she refused to let it in. Despite all her thoughts to the contrary, she had to think of Wade as just a friend.

Chapter Eleven

A chorus of cicadas accompanied the sound of the ocean as Wade walked to Cassie's town house. The rain, lingering on the grass, dampened his shoes and made them shine in the moonlight. Even though the vertical blinds covering the patio doors were drawn, a light still shone through her window and fell on the patio—a good indication that she was still up. It wasn't late, but would she appreciate a visitor now?

Why was he doing this? Hadn't it been just hours since he'd seen her? Wasn't he going to see her in the morning? But he hadn't been able to get Cassie or the kids out of his mind all evening, especially the episode with Jack. Wade's dinner companions had caught him daydreaming several times during the meal. Each time he'd been thinking of Cassie or the kids.

He hesitated on the patio, before knocking. He hoped he wouldn't scare her by coming to this door. Maybe he should go around to the front and ring the doorbell. While he wavered back and forth about what he should do, the patio light came on. He stepped back when the blinds parted and Cassie appeared at the doorway. Had she heard him make a noise and come to inspect the source? Did she see him now?

After she opened the door and stepped out onto the patio, he softly called, "Cassie."

She jerked her head his way. "What are you doing here?"

Her words didn't seem accusatory, just curious. "I hope I didn't frighten you. I was just coming over to see how your evening went. I was worried about Jack."

"You frightened me for a moment, until I recognized you."

"Sorry."

"I never expected to see you this evening. I thought you had a date."

Wade chuckled. "Hardly a date. I went out to eat with some of the guys I know from work. It was a kind of get-to-know you dinner."

"Oh, that's nice."

"Yeah, it was," Wade replied, thinking there was a hint of relief in Cassie's voice. Was she glad it hadn't been a date? Man. He was definitely indulging in wishful thinking. He needed a better topic to occupy his mind. "How were the kids tonight? Tired from the beach?"

"Yeah. They went right to bed without a fuss. Even Makayla. They're all asleep now." Cassie held something up for him to see. "A baby monitor that Angie bought for me. I put it in Jack and Danny's room."

"That's a good idea, when you want to come out here while they're sleeping."

"Yeah, I love to sit out here and listen to the sound of the ocean. It's so peaceful and soothing."

"And you deserve some quiet time for yourself." He turned to go. "So I won't disturb you."

Cassie stepped closer and touched his arm. "You don't have to leave. I like having adult company."

Trying to read her expression, he looked back at her. She stood silhouetted against the light coming from inside, as well as the patio light, so he couldn't see her face. "Okay. I just wanted to make sure I wasn't intruding."

"You're not intruding at all." She sat on one of the lounge chairs and indicated that he should sit in the chair next to hers.

Glancing at the chair, he wondered whether this was the right thing to do. She was asking him to stay. Wasn't that what he wanted? But at the same time, his attraction to her made him want to run scared. He didn't want to get hurt again, and he didn't want to see the pity on her face when she learned about his battle with cancer. Was he even brave enough to bring up the subject? He doubted he was. He wanted to be a healthy, whole man who could give her everything she deserved.

Finally, he sat on the other lounge chair. For a few moments, they sat without speaking, while the sound of waves crashing to shore filled the silence. He didn't look her way, but stared straight ahead at the dunes. "I felt really bad about Jack this afternoon. I never dreamed our game would upset him."

"Me, neither."

"Did he mention it again?"

"No, but Makayla did. She kept telling him that he shouldn't have hit you." Cassie sighed. "My sister said Darrell never beat her, but after what happened with Jack today, I'm wondering whether that was all a lie."

"Jack certainly was upset." Wade looked at Cassie. "Do you have any communication with your sister?"

"No. I know I should visit her, but the thought frightens me. I can't imagine going to visit someone in prison."

"Maybe there's a prison ministry that could help you."

"I'm not sure she would be receptive to anything religious."

"You never know. Maybe being in prison will soften her heart."

"Or harden it further."

"We should definitely pray about it."

Cassie sighed again. "I'm not sure how, or what to pray for."

"We can just pray that somehow God would send someone into her life."

"You're right. I've seen that in my own life. I believe God sent Angie into mine. Sam needs someone like Angie."

"You should put your sister on the prayer list at church."

"I'm not sure I want people to know I have a sister in prison."

"But how do you explain having your sister's children?"

"I don't."

"Even when someone asks?"

"I just say I'm taking care of them, and people don't ask beyond that."

"Well, it wouldn't hurt to let others know about your situation. They would certainly pray for you, the kids and your sister."

"I suppose you're right, but I feel as though people will look down on me. My bad family reflects on me."

Wade shook his head. "No one can blame you for what your family has done."

Cassie shrugged. "I just don't want to take the chance."

"Do you believe I think badly of you because of your family?"

Cassie turned her head and stared at him, almost as if she couldn't believe he'd asked the question. Her eyes opened wide. "Do you?"

"No, I admire you for taking on the responsibility of your nieces and nephews."

She leaned forward. "You do?"

"Of course. You're doing a wonderful thing." Wade wished he had the courage to tell her how much he cared. Their age difference stuck in his mind and made him a coward. And then there was his cancer. Here he was telling her to open up her life for the church prayer list, when he couldn't even tell her about his past health problems. He ought to follow his own advice.

Why couldn't he open up to her the way she did with him? But she probably had no trouble telling him about her life, because she considered him someone older who would listen to her problems. While he was entertaining romantic ideas, she was using him as a sounding board.

"I don't think of it as something special. It's the only thing I could do to keep the kids together. I want them to have a better childhood than I had."

"And they will.

Cassie looked back toward the dunes. "I don't know. Sometimes it's so hard to do the right thing."

"No parents are perfect. They all make mistakes."

"And then there are the really bad ones, like my parents. Sometimes I worry that I'll be just like them."

"Never."

"You believe that, even after I swore at the kids?"

Wade nodded. "Yes. Even though you swore at them, you apologized. You just made a mistake."

"I bet *your* parents didn't make mistakes."

Wade laughed halfheartedly. "My parents made plenty of mistakes, but my brothers and I always knew they loved us. That was the important thing."

"Oh, I do love these kids."

"And it shows."

"I hope so. I'm a little worried about the next visit from the caseworker. What will Jack say about the water fight at the beach?"

"I didn't think about that. Will it be a problem?"

"I'm not sure."

"Would you like me to stay away for a while?"

Even in the dim light, Wade read the dismay on her face. "Oh, no! Makayla and Taylor bombard me with questions during the week. 'Is Mr. Wade home? Is Mr. Wade going to have lunch with us? When is Mr. Wade going to play with us on the beach?' They'd be so disappointed if you suddenly weren't around."

"That's nice to know, but I hope Jack won't continue to think I'm the bad guy," Wade said, wondering whether Cassie missed him the way the little girls did.

"We'll have to see how things go tomorrow." Cassie looked at him with a shy smile almost like Taylor's. "I'm looking forward to our picnic."

"Me, too." Wade hoped her eagerness for the outing meant she enjoyed his company, as well. Was that too much to ask?

After paying the fee at the ranger station, Wade drove his SUV slowly down a road shaded by a tree canopy of live oaks draped with Spanish moss. It was hard to believe they would find a Civil War fort at the end of this picturesque drive. It was also hard to believe how much he enjoyed being with these kids and their aunt— especially their aunt. His admiration for her grew every time they were together. He just wasn't sure how he was going to deal with the emotional attachment he'd formed with them all.

"When do we get to the fort?" Makayla asked as she strained against her seat belt. "All I see are trees."

Cassie turned to look at Makayla in the backseat. "We'll be there in a few minutes. Just be patient."

"I wanna see the cannons." Jack puffed out his chest as if he were trying to play soldier.

"First we're going to have lunch, then we'll tour the fort." Wade drove his SUV into a parking lot. "We're here. Everybody out."

"Is that the fort?" Jack pointed at a nearby brick building.

"No, that's the visitor center." Cassie helped Danny out of his car seat and picked him up.

Makayla and Taylor helped Wade get the picnic basket out of the rear of the vehicle.

"Where do we eat?" Makayla asked.

Cassie pointed to a sign at the edge of the parking lot. "We take that trail right over there."

"Yippee!" Makayla skipped ahead.

Taylor and Jack hurried to catch up. Carrying the food they'd picked up at KFC, Wade walked side-by-side with Cassie as they traversed the pine-needle-covered path.

"The kids were very good in church this morning," Wade said.

Cassie nodded. "That was a blessing. They're getting used to the routine. And their Bible-school teachers are really great with the kids. They look forward to the classes, especially Taylor. That child is very eager to learn. I hope she'll always feel that way. I'm glad you suggested this outing. It'll be educational, as well as fun."

"I hope so," Wade said, wishing Cassie would see this outing as more than just a good thing for the kids. Was there any way to make her look at him in a context separate from the children?

In a minute, they'd reached the picnic area. Several picnic tables were scattered in the shade of the live oaks. A jungle gym sat off to one side. Makayla and Jack headed directly to the playground equipment.

Makayla started to climb the ladder to one of the numerous slides. "Watch me go down."

"Not until you eat lunch. Come back over here now." Cassie set Danny on one of the benches of the picnic table.

Stopping halfway up the ladder, Makayla made a face. "Why is everything after we eat?"

"To make sure you have a good lunch. Please come back over here." Pointing at the table, Cassie gave Makayla a stern look. "I mean *right now*."

Scowling, Makayla came down the ladder and shuffled to the table. Jack followed her without protest, while Taylor helped Wade and Cassie spread a cloth on the table. Then all the older kids helped to bring out the food from the picnic basket.

After everything was ready, Makayla settled on the bench next to Taylor and announced, "I'm going to eat everything."

"I hope not everything, since the rest of us would like to eat, too." Cassie slid onto the bench next to Wade.

Makayla laughed. "I didn't mean everything. I meant a little bit of everything."

"That's good to know. I was beginning to think I wouldn't get anything to eat." Wade patted her on the head.

"Mr. Wade and Aunt Cassie, you're being silly." Taylor put her hands over her mouth and giggled.

Seeing Taylor's amusement made him even more aware of how much Cassie was doing for these children. The shy little girl he'd met when he first arrived on the island was coming out of her shell more and more with each passing day. "You're right, Taylor. We're being sort of silly to think Makayla could eat all the food."

Still smiling, Taylor nodded. "She'd get sick if she ate it all, wouldn't she?"

Wade handed the girl a bright red plastic plate and utensils. "You've got that right."

Wade said a blessing, and then everyone started eating the fried chicken, baked beans and coleslaw. While they ate, several other groups came to the picnic area and occupied the other tables. Laughter and conversation filtered through the wooded area. Wade took in the happiness and peace that surrounded him in this setting. His cancer had been gone for months, but the emotional scars had lingered until Cassie and her charges came into his life. They'd made him look beyond himself. Their presence had brought a new contentment to him.

After the children finished their lunches, Cassie took them over to the jungle gym. Taylor and Makayla went down the slide, while Cassie pushed Jack in the swing. As Wade gathered the trash and repacked the picnic basket, he marveled that this young woman could manage these four children. She performed a delicate balancing act that he was sure he could never duplicate.

He shouldn't be surprised. He'd witnessed it time and time again when they were together. And he was astonished that she didn't think taking in her nieces and nephews was anything extraordinary, that it was something special for a twenty-one-year-old to do.

How could he become part of this picture? What would happen if he asked her for a date? Had he been using the kids as an excuse to be with her? The troubling questions floated through his mind like the hawk circling high above them. The questions continued to plague him as he joined Cassie and the children at the jungle gym.

While they played, he tried not to think about wanting to be part of this family. He'd given up on the idea of a family after the cancer had pushed away the woman who had promised to marry him. But after seeing the way Cassie dealt with the children, he thought she might be different. Was he right? Right now, he wasn't sure he had the courage to find out.

Cassie helped Danny go down the slide, then turned to the rest of the children. "Okay, kids, one last slide for everyone. Then it's off to the fort."

Jack hurried to take his turn. "I'm gonna see cannons."

Holding Danny, Cassie looked down at the older children. "Now, when we get into the fort, I don't want you to run off on your own. You stay with Mr. Wade and me. Do you understand?"

"Yes, ma'am," they said, their heads bobbing up and down.

"Okay, then. Let's go." Cassie started across the parking lot to the visitor center.

Wade held the door open while Cassie and the kids filed into the building. He went to the counter and paid the entry fee to get into the fort. The children were fascinated with the trinkets and souvenirs on display in the gift shop.

Makayla held up a toy soldier. "I want one of these."

"No, Makayla, you can't have that," Cassie said.

"Why?" she whined.

"Because you don't have the money to buy it." Cassie took it and put it back on the shelf.

Makayla stamped her foot. "But I want it."

"If you don't quit complaining, I'll take you to the car, and Mr. Wade will take everyone else inside the fort. You won't get to go."

"Okay, I'll be good." Makayla scampered to stand next to Taylor and Jack, who were ready to go through the door leading to the fort.

Cassie looked at Wade, as if she wanted reassurance that she'd done the right thing. "Are you ready?"

Stepping closer to her, he had a sudden protective feeling toward her. He wanted to take away all her anxiety, but with four little children to care for, that was not going to happen. Kids and anxiety went hand in hand. But at least he could help lighten the load. "Would you like me to carry Danny for a while?"

She looked up at him with a smile. "That would be great."

Wade reached out his hands, and Danny went willingly into his arms. Wade tried to concentrate on the toddler, rather than on the way his heart tripped when Cassie smiled at him like that. Her smile had him doing things he would never have dreamed of doing just weeks ago. He was taking care of a toddler, buying gifts for kids and falling for an incredible young woman.

As they went through the door, Danny laid his head on Wade's shoulder. He glanced down at the child and realized he cared about him, too. He cared about them all. What was he going to do about it?

They walked through the entrance. Red brick and mortar formed the exterior walls of the fort. As they crossed the wooden bridge at the entrance, Wade stopped. "Hey, kids, look at this. A drawbridge and moat, just like we put in our sandcastle."

"But why isn't there any water in the moat?" Makayla asked.

"Look at all the cannons!" Jack's exclamation rescued Wade from having to answer Makayla's question. "Do they still shoot the cannons?"

"No, those are very old, and they're just for show now," Cassie replied.

Jack's eyes grew wide. "Can I touch them?"

"Sure. Let's go up the ramp over there to get to the top." Cassie took Jack's hand and led him up the concrete ramp to the top of the rampart where the cannons sat.

When they got there, Jack, Taylor and Makayla raced

each other to the cannons. Jack reached up his little hand to touch a cannon, but he was too short, so Cassie picked him up. As he put his hand on the big, black cannon, he smiled as if he'd accomplished some huge feat.

Makayla pointed to the body of water visible from where they stood. "Is that the ocean, like where we live?"

"No, that's Cumberland Sound." Cassie hunkered down and directed their attention across the water. "Do you see that land over there?"

Makayla nodded. "Yes, ma'am."

"That's Cumberland Island. It's in Georgia, and there are wild horses over there."

"Can we go over there sometime and see the wild horses?" Taylor asked.

"Maybe. You can only get there by going on a boat. There's no bridge like we have here." Cassie stood and motioned for them to move on. "Okay, kids, let's explore the rest of the fort."

Wade put Danny up on his shoulders as they walked around the entire fort where the cannons were stationed. The kids went up and down the staircases built of brick and mortar. They looked through rifle ports and visited the barracks, guardhouse, bakery, blacksmith shop, storehouse, officers' kitchen, and dispensary, with its display of historic medical instruments.

When they went into the quartermaster's store, a historic interpreter, dressed as a union soldier, greeted them and said, "Uniforms come in two sizes. Too big and too small."

Wide-eyed, Jack stared at the man as he continued in his role. After they left the building, Jack tapped Wade on the arm. "Was that a real soldier?"

Wade smiled. "No, he was just playing one, but he seemed pretty real, didn't he?"

"Yeah," Jack replied, awe coloring his voice.

Finally, they exited the fort through the visitor center, where Wade read some of the displays explaining the history of the fort, built to protect the entrance to St. Mary's River and the harbor of Fernandina. When they got to the parking lot, Wade opened the back of his SUV. Cassie grabbed several colorful plastic pails, sifters and shovels.

"What are we doing now?" Makayla asked.

"Miss Angie said we should look for shark teeth on the beach." Cassie pointed to an unpaved road. "If we go down this road, we'll come to the beach."

"Will we see sharks?" Taylor asked. "I don't want to see sharks. They're scary."

"No sharks, but real shark teeth."

"Cool." Makayla skipped alongside of Cassie. "What do they look like?"

"They're usually black and shaped like a triangle. Angie said to walk along the water's edge and we might see some. If not, we can sift through the sand with these." Cassie handed out shovels and sifters for everyone.

When they reached the end of the road, Jack yelled as he pointed toward the thick brick walls rising from the sandy beach. "I see the fort and the cannons again!"

Meandering down the beach, Cassie and the three older children had their heads bowed as they searched the sand for shark teeth. Danny was more interested in chasing the birds that gathered near the surf. Wade lagged behind as he tried to sort out his emotions. Today's outing had crystallized his feelings about

Cassie and the kids more than he'd anticipated. He tried to imagine his life without them, and he couldn't. But how did she view him? He didn't want to be just the friendly neighbor, but he wasn't sure how to change the status quo.

Taylor held up something in her hand. "I think I found one!"

Cassie went to examine her find. "You certainly have."

Makayla and Jack gathered around to look at Taylor's treasure. Wade scooped Danny up in his arms, and the little boy giggled as the two of them went to join the group. The sound of the child's delight warmed Wade's heart and further cemented the idea of making Cassie and the kids a permanent part of his life. What a crazy idea, when he hadn't even taken any steps to find out how Cassie felt.

They had spent a number of weekends in each other's company, but none of their time together had been spent in the context of a date. He had to do something to change that. He still feared rejection, but if he wanted her in his life, he had to take some action to make it happen. He couldn't continue to hide behind his role as a neighbor.

"Mr. Wade, do you like my shark tooth?"

Taylor's question shook him from his thoughts. He looked down at the girl, who beamed with pride as she held it up. "That's great."

"How come I can't find one?" Makayla whined.

"You just have to keep looking." Cassie patted Makayla on the head. "You'll find one."

"I'll help you, Makayla," Taylor said.

Eventually, they found enough shark teeth for each

child to have some, then headed back to Wade's SUV. After they'd stowed their paraphernalia, all the kids hopped into their seats, and Cassie buckled them in. With the air conditioning blowing full blast, Wade started to back out of the parking spot. As he slowly drove away, a commotion broke out in the backseat.

"What's going on back there?" Cassie asked, as she turned to look at Taylor and Makayla.

Taylor pointed at her sister. "She took something from the shop."

Cassie motioned to Wade. "Please stop." Then she looked back at the two girls. "Okay, tell me what's going on here."

Taylor tried to grab something Makayla held tight in one fist. "You said she couldn't have that toy soldier in the shop, but she took it."

"Makayla, did you do that?" Cassie asked.

Makayla pressed her lips together as she hunched her shoulders. She pulled her hand away and hid it behind her back. Shaking her head, she refused to say anything.

Cassie reached into the backseat. "Please show me what you've got."

Still shaking her head, Makayla continued to hide her hand behind her back.

"If you don't show it to me, I'll have to come back there."

Makayla still wouldn't obey. Sighing, Cassie unbuckled her seat belt and opened the door. Before she stepped out of the vehicle, Makayla started to cry.

"Please don't hurt me. Here it is." She held out her hand, showing the little blue-uniformed soldier.

Cassie opened the door to the backseat. "I'm not going to hurt you, but you have to take this back to the gift shop."

Makayla hung her head and sniffled. "What will they do to me?"

"I don't know what they'll do, but you have to take it back." Cassie helped Makayla out of the SUV.

Wade pulled back into a parking spot. He waited with the other children, while Cassie escorted a sobbing Makayla into the visitor center.

"Are they going to put Makayla in jail?" Jack asked.

Wade turned and looked at the little boy. "No, they aren't going to put her in jail, but she's going to be in trouble. You know better than to take something from a store without paying, don't you?"

"Yes, sir," Jack said, bobbing his head up and down.

"She did a bad thing," Taylor said, with a hint of superiority painting her words.

Wade wasn't sure how to respond to Taylor's comment. The simple answer was yes, but he didn't want to give her the idea that she was somehow better than her sister. This situation only served to show him again that Cassie had taken on a very difficult job. Caring for her meant being part of that task. Was he ready for that? Was it what he wanted?

Chapter Twelve

The waves of heat coming off the parking lot seemed to suffocate Cassie as she dragged Makayla back to Wade's SUV. The little girl continued to sniffle and wipe her nose and eyes with a tissue. What a mess! Wade surely thought they were a bunch of bad apples. At least the lady in charge of the gift shop had been sympathetic. She'd been very understanding with Makayla, who'd sobbed through the entire exercise of returning the little soldier. Cassie just hoped the trauma of having to admit her wrongdoing would stick with the little girl and keep her from repeating the mistake.

Then there was the matter of punishment. Cassie had to walk a fine line there. She didn't want to remind the child of the abuse that had come from her mother and stepfather, so being sent to her room was out of the question. But the child needed to have some consequences for what she'd done. Grounding her would be the logical answer, but how could that be done without involving the other children? She couldn't very well leave Makayla by herself while the others went to the beach or the pool. How was she going to accomplish this task?

When Cassie and Makayla got back, they got in and buckled their seat belts. Cassie glanced over at Wade, who raised his eyebrows in a questioning look.

Before Cassie said anything, Jack blurted, "Did Makayla get whupped? Mr. Wade said they wouldn't put her in jail."

Despite the seriousness of the situation, Jack's question nearly made Cassie giggle. She bit her bottom lip and shook her head as she continued to look at Wade. His eyes twinkled, and she could tell he was also fighting back a smile. She shouldn't have been worried that he wouldn't understand. The more she was around him, the more she longed to have him there to depend on all of the time. Was that an impossible dream?

Cassie pushed the thought away as she looked at Jack. "No, she didn't get whupped. She had to apologize for taking the toy, and she had to promise never to do that again."

"Makayla did a bad thing. Makayla did a bad thing," Jack chanted.

Cassie gave him a stern look. "Jack, that's enough. She said she was sorry. Now we're not going to talk about it anymore. Do you understand?"

He hung his head. "Yes, ma'am."

During the rest of the ride home, the children were quiet. Wade turned on the radio, and uplifting music from a Christian radio station in Jacksonville filled the air. Cassie relaxed as she let the words of the song, about putting trust in the Lord, capture her thoughts.

Why was she always trying to do things on her own and not remembering to trust God? Old habits were hard to break.

When they arrived home, Wade pulled into his garage. Cassie hopped out of the SUV, unbuckled Danny and lifted him from his car seat. The other children scrambled out and chased each other around on the grass between the two driveways, the episode at the fort seemingly forgotten.

Cassie looked back at Wade as he walked out of the garage. "Thanks for taking us on the picnic. I'm sorry about Makayla's problem. I never dreamed she would take that thing when I told her she couldn't have it."

"You don't have to thank me. And don't worry about Makayla. I think she learned her lesson."

"Maybe. I'd really like to ground her, but I don't know how to do that without punishing the other kids as well."

"I might be able to help."

"I'm not expecting you to deal with this. It's not your problem."

"But I'd like to help. What if I take the other kids for ice cream, and Makayla doesn't get to go?"

Cassie remembered how Makayla had asked whether they could go for ice cream. Would this work? "Are you sure?"

"I wouldn't have asked if I wasn't." He gave her a crooked grin. "I admire the way you've handled the situation."

Wade's praise made her feel warm all over. "When would you like to do this?" she asked.

"Now?"

Cassie glanced down at Danny. "He's getting tired.

I'm afraid if you took him now, he'd become really cranky. Then you'd be sorry you took them."

"What do you suggest?"

"He needs a nap. All the kids need some quiet time. Maybe after supper?" Cassie hoped he didn't think she was taking advantage of his willingness to help.

"Okay. I can see he's getting sleepy. Besides, I have some reports I need to work on." Wade rubbed the top of Danny's head. "How about if I fix hot dogs on my grill for supper?"

"You don't have to do that."

"Cassie, if I suggest it, I don't mind doing it. Believe me—I enjoy your company. Come on over about five-thirty."

"Okay." she said, trying not to read too much into his invitation.

After Wade served supper, he took Taylor, Jack and Danny for ice cream. Makayla cried and ran to her room when she learned she couldn't go with the others. Cassie had to force herself not to relent and let her go. Being a disciplinarian wasn't easy. While Cassie sat in the living room and tried to block the sound of the crying child from her mind, the doorbell rang. Was Wade back already? She hurried to the door and opened it.

Angie stood on the porch. "Hi, I stopped by to see how you're doing."

"Oh, things could be better," Cassie said as she opened the door. What would Angie think when she heard about Makayla?

Angie gave her a quizzical look. "Problems?"

Cassie explained what had happened during their

time at the fort and how Makayla had been excluded from getting ice cream, then waited for Angie's reaction.

"I think you handled that very well." Angie surveyed the room. "Where is she now?"

"As soon as the others left, she ran up to her bedroom and flung herself on the bed and sobbed her little heart out."

"She'll get over it."

"I know she will, but it's hard to listen to that."

Angie patted Cassie on the arm. "Let's talk about something happy."

"And what's that?"

"My company's one of the sponsors of a charity dinner here at the Ritz in a couple of weeks. I want you to go."

Looking at Angie in dismay, Cassie shook her head. "I can't go to your charity dinner. I…I won't fit in."

"That's nonsense." Angie waved her hand at Cassie. "You'll fit in just like the next person. It's a lovely dinner at the Ritz, for a good cause, and I'm paying. So no argument."

"The Ritz is too fancy for me. And all those people have lots of money and education." Cassie sighed heavily. "What would I say to them? I'd sound like a country bumpkin. As soon as I opened my mouth, they'd know I don't belong."

"You can go with Wade. You can talk to him all night."

Cassie stared wide-eyed at Angie. "With Wade? That's even worse. He'd be embarrassed to be with me."

"Cassandra Rankin, quit putting yourself down. You're a lovely young woman. I'm sure Wade will be quite proud to have you as his date."

"Date? You never said anything about a date. Did you tell Wade this was a date?"

Shaking her head, Angie grinned. "I haven't said a thing to him."

"Well, good, then we won't have to bother him," Cassie said. Despite her protests, she felt an odd anxiety that maybe Wade wouldn't want to go. Deep down inside she wished Angie had already made the arrangements with him.

"I'll talk to him tonight when he gets back."

"What would I do with the kids?"

"I'll find a babysitter."

"That might be difficult, when you tell them it's for four little kids."

"Let me worry about it."

"Are you sure Wade will agree to go? I don't want him to feel obligated."

"It won't hurt him." Angie patted Cassie on the arm. "Now quit trying to find reasons not to go."

"I can't help it. I don't have anything to wear."

"Yes, you do. Wait right here." Angie hurried out to her car and returned holding a garment bag. "Come with me."

"Before I do, let me check on Makayla."

"Okay, meet me in your bedroom."

Cassie hurried up the stairs and found that Makayla had cried herself to sleep. Her heart ached for the little girl. At times she saw so much of herself in this child. She didn't ever want to dampen her enthusiasm for life.

When Cassie got back to her bedroom, Angie asked, "How is she?"

"Asleep. I sure hope she won't be cranky when she wakes up."

"She'll be fine."

"What's in there?" Cassie asked as she observed the garment bag on the bed.

"Your dress, Cinderella." Angie unzipped the bag, lifted a flowing red dress out of the bag and held it up. "Try it on. I promise it won't turn into rags at midnight."

Smiling, Cassie came closer and fingered the red chiffon, which overlaid the satin beneath it and hung in a tiered hemline. She'd never owned, or even tried on, such a beautiful dress. Despite all her misgivings about Angie's plan, Cassie wanted to try on the exquisite gown. Taking a deep breath, she took the hanger and held the dress in front of herself. She gazed in the mirror, then glanced at Angie. "You didn't buy this just for me, did you?"

"No, actually, it belongs to the daughter of a friend of mine. I knew she was about the same size as you, so I asked if I could borrow one of her special-occasion dresses."

"And she didn't mind lending out her dress?"

"She won't even miss it. She has a closet full of party dresses."

Cassie couldn't imagine. The idea of a closet full of dresses of any kind just reminded her that this event would be filled with well-to-do people. The kind of people she wouldn't feel comfortable around. "What if it doesn't fit or doesn't look good on me?"

"Then we'll look for another one." Angie shooed her into the adjoining bathroom. "Now try it on. I'm sure you'll be gorgeous in it."

Cassie closed the door and hung the dress on the hook on the inside. Taking off her shorts and T-shirt, she stared at the dress. She wanted it to fit so she could go to the party. She wanted Wade to look at her and see a beautiful woman. Maybe she could have at least one of those wishes.

She took the dress off the hanger and slipped it over her head. Smoothing it into place, she let her hand linger on the soft material. She felt like a princess, even without looking in the mirror. Finally she lifted her gaze to see her image. The dress did everything she'd hoped it would.

"How's it going in there?" Angie asked. "Do you need some help? May I come in?"

Cassie turned the doorknob and let the door swing open as she stood there in her bare feet, her arms held wide. "What do you think?"

"Oh, Cassie, you're gorgeous in that dress. You'll be the envy of every woman in the room. And you'll dazzle all the men."

"I'm not interested in dazzling men." Cassie wanted only to dazzle one man. *Was that possible?*

Angie smiled and gave Cassie a hug. "But you *are* interested in capturing the interest of Wade Dalton."

"How'd you know that?" Cassie worried that if Angie recognized her interest, he would, too.

"I've seen the way you look at him."

"How do I look at him? Do I stare?" she asked, fearing he had noticed that look.

Patting Cassie's arm, Angie chuckled. "No, but your eyes light up when he walks into the room."

"But I don't want him to know."

"You're kidding yourself if you think that's true."

"Okay, you're right. I do want him to know, but I want him to feel the same way."

"Believe me, Cassie, he won't know what hit him when he sees you in that red dress. I can hardly wait."

"Are you sure? To him I'm just his neighbor—a friend."

"Once he looks at you in this dress, he'll think of you as more than a friend."

"I don't know. Whenever I get too friendly, he backs away. He's been hurt before."

Angie raised her eyebrows. "He told you that?"

"Well, not exactly. He told me he'd been engaged and his fiancée broke the engagement. So I just figured he must've been hurt."

"Did he tell you why?"

"No. He doesn't seem to like to talk much about himself."

"I have a feeling things might change after this event."

"Do you really think a man like Wade could have an interest in me? After all, he's way older."

"Age isn't going to make a difference."

"But I'm so afraid he thinks of me as one of the kids next door."

Angie shook her head. "I don't think the man sees you as a kid. Believe me. And after he gets a look at you in this dress, he'll definitely see a woman, not a kid."

"I'm not sure I'm ready for this."

"Yes, you are." Angie snapped her fingers. "Now we need to see about getting some shoes to go with that dress. And they *won't* be glass slippers."

Wade combed his hair and tried to tell himself he wasn't nervous. Why should he be nervous? He'd spent hours and hours with Cassie and never been nervous. Maybe tongue-tied a couple of times, when they'd first met and he'd been overwhelmed by her generosity, but never nervous. But tonight was different. Tonight was a date. Yeah, a date. An arranged one, but still a date.

They'd spent almost the entire Fourth of July weekend together, knowing they would attend this dinner, but they hadn't talked about it once. Their focus had been on the kids and the excitement of the holiday weekend.

On the Fourth of July, they'd sat on the beach and watched the airplanes making acrobatic maneuvers and skywriting over the ocean. They'd grilled hot dogs and hamburgers and made homemade ice cream. During the evening, they'd stood on the dunes walkover and watched the fireworks going off up and down the beach, first from the Ritz-Carlton and then from Amelia Island Plantation and, in the distance, the fireworks from the north end of the island.

Wade had a feeling those fireworks couldn't compete with the fireworks going off inside him when he thought about taking Cassie to this dinner.

Now that it was here, the reality of this date hit him. The opportunity he'd been waiting for had been dropped in his lap. Angie's invitation had come at the perfect time. Did he dare believe it was the answer to his prayers? He'd believed at one time that God had brought Julia and him together, and that relationship had fallen apart. So he wasn't sure what to make of the unlikely combination of Cassie and him and four little kids. Was this just something he wanted, or was this something God had in mind? Wade had to admit he didn't always understand God's plan for his life.

As the day drew closer, he had finally discussed the evening with Cassie, the same way they had discussed so many outings with the kids. So why should he be nervous? Because she didn't seem all that excited, while he felt like a teenager going on his first date. What had Angie had in mind when she asked him to take Cassie, other than selling two more tickets to the charity event? Was she matchmaking, or was Cassie going on the date just to do Angie a favor? Oh, he had to quit analyzing the evening and just go over and get Cassie.

As he walked to her front door, he passed the babysitter's car. He ran a finger around the inside of his collar. Even though he'd adjusted his tie earlier, he suddenly felt as though it was too tight. The warm night air was suffocating, or was it just a product of his anxiety?

Taking a deep breath, he rang the doorbell. He shifted his weight from foot to foot while he waited for what seemed like hours for her to answer the door.

The door opened. He swallowed hard as he took in the sight of Cassie in the most elegant red dress he'd ever seen. Sunlight glinted off the gold earrings dangling from her ears. A gold choker with some kind of bauble hung around her neck. Maybe it wasn't so much the dress or the jewelry as the beautiful woman *in* the dress. He didn't think she could be any lovelier.

Then she smiled.

Nothing could have prepared him for the impact of her smile. He hoped he hadn't been standing there with his mouth open. Finally, managing to speak, he said, "Hi, ready to go?"

"I am, but the kids want to see you."

"Okay." He followed Cassie into the town house. "You look really nice tonight."

"Thanks," she said without turning around. As she walked, the material of the dress floated around her legs.

He wanted to go to the door again and start all over. Why hadn't he said how great she looked when she first opened the door? And why had he said *tonight,* as if she'd never looked good before? She looked more than nice, but he had been too overwhelmed to come up with the right adjective.

When he walked into the living room, the three older children were sitting on the couch watching a video. A white-haired lady sat in a nearby chair and bounced Danny on her knee.

Makayla jumped up as soon as he entered the room, but Cassie motioned for her to sit down while she introduced Wade to Mrs. Warren, the babysitter, who lived in one of the patio homes down the street.

Unable to contain her excitement, Makayla jumped up again. "Mr. Wade, you look really handsome."

"Thank you, Makayla."

"Aunt Cassie looks like a princess," Taylor said in a dreamy voice. "And you look like a prince."

Standing, Mrs. Warren smiled. "You two handsome young people run along now. The kids and I will have a great evening, and you will, too."

"Y'all be good for Mrs. Warren." Cassie opened her arms wide. "Hugs before I go."

The children clamored to give Cassie kisses and hugs. The little girls gave Wade a hug, but Jack shook his hand. Where had the little boy seen that?

"Okay. Let's go, or we'll be late." Feeling a little more relaxed, Wade ushered Cassie out the door.

Without talking, they walked to his driveway, and he opened the door to his SUV and helped her inside. Driving the short distance to the Ritz-Carlton, he searched for something to talk about. A dozen things sifted through his mind, but they all seemed completely trivial. Maybe he should start with something clichéd, like the weather. At least he would end the silence. "Did you see on the news about the latest tropical storm?"

"No." She glanced his way. "What did they say about it?"

"Right now they think it'll develop into a hurricane, but probably not for several days."

"Do they have any predictions on its path?"

"Right now they're showing Florida."

"Close to us?" Cassie bit her bottom lip.

"We're in the watch area, but you know how that goes. Seems like so many of those hurricanes make a turn north and eventually hit somewhere in the Carolinas."

"Yeah, I've seen that pattern over and over again, but it always makes me nervous when they're out there."

"It can be unsettling," Wade agreed, remembering how much even thunderstorms worried Cassie.

He turned into the drive leading to the Ritz-Carlton. An array of pink, white, red and violet impatiens covered the median and lined both sides of the drive. Palm trees stood like sentinels guarding the property, and sprawling live oaks cast shadows across the median. A huge fountain at the entrance spilled water from level to level.

Wade drove under the portico, and immediately a young man was there to open Cassie's door. Wade didn't miss the expression of awe on the young man's face when Cassie stepped from the vehicle. After giving the valet his keys, Wade hurried to claim Cassie. Smiling up at him, she slipped her arm through his. He was the happiest man alive with her walking by his side.

"Where are we supposed to meet Angie?" Cassie asked as the doorman greeted them.

Wade glanced around at the rich wood paneling that covered the walls. "Right here in the lobby."

"There you two are." Angie, dressed in a stunning black dress, came bustling toward them. "I'll show you where the dinner is."

As they followed Angie down a wide corridor, Wade felt Cassie's grip on his arm tighten. Maybe she was as nervous as he was about this date. Neither of them should be nervous, because they'd spent hours together. But this outing gave a new dimension to their relationship. They had gone beyond friendship. Where would it lead?

When they reached the ballroom where the dinner was being held, Angie introduced them to several people. Then she went to mingle with some of the other guests. Wade started chatting with two of the couples they'd just met. Cassie hung back in silence. Wade had never seen her so reticent.

An older gentlemen with neatly styled gray hair stepped forward and motioned toward Cassie. "And what do you do, young lady?"

Her eyes grew wide, and Wade could read the angst in her expression and sensed her nervousness as she tried to hold a smile in place. "I work for an insurance agency in town."

The man nodded. "You could be in for some busy times, with that hurricane spinning away out there in the Caribbean."

"It's a hurricane already? I thought it was just a tropical storm," Wade commented, hoping to draw attention away from Cassie until she felt more comfortable.

"I saw it on the news just before we left the house. It had been upgraded to a minimal hurricane and was heading this way."

"So you really think it'll hit this area? These early predictions always seem to be wrong," a stylishly coifed woman in a blue gown said with a wave of her hand.

"I suppose you're right." The older gentleman nodded. "It's too early to tell. I still remember the evacuation for Hurricane Floyd. What a mess. We were on the road for hours and only got a few miles."

"And then it didn't hit here. All that for nothing." Shaking her head, the woman grimaced. "It's too bad they can't make more accurate predictions. These false alarms make people less cautious."

"But you know the whole island has a mandatory evacuation for a category one hurricane now?" Cassie said.

"Yes, I'd heard that," Wade replied, glad to see Cassie voluntarily join in on the conversation. She appeared a little less apprehensive now.

"We ought to know something more definite in a week or so." Wade smiled at Cassie. "I hope it just turns away from land and languishes out in the North Atlantic."

"That would definitely be the best scenario," the older man agreed.

While the group continued to discuss the threat of hurricanes in the area, a young man with dark brown hair, who looked to be near Cassie's age, approached them. "Cassie Rankin, is that you?"

Cassie looked up at him and grinned. "Jordan Wagner, what are you doing here?"

"I'm one of Angie Clark's project superintendents."

He gave Cassie a hug and then stepped back to admire her. "You look terrific in that dress."

Cassie beamed. "Thanks."

"I haven't seen you since your brother Harlan joined the army. Where are you living now?"

"On the island, just a little ways from here."

"Are you working here?"

Cassie nodded. "For an insurance agency."

Wade followed the conversation with a growing sense of dismay. When Cassie spotted the younger man, her face had lit up. She'd suddenly become animated and lost all her former reserve. She seemed to have forgotten he was even there. Why hadn't he told her she looked terrific in that dress? Now some young guy had captured her attention. That told him what his status was with her—the old guy who had been foisted on her for the evening.

"Wade," Cassie said, touching his arm. "I want you to meet someone. This is Jordan Wagner. He's a friend of my brother Harlan. They went to high school together."

"Nice to meet you. I'm Cassie's neighbor." As he shook the younger man's hand, Wade wished he'd identified himself as Cassie's date. But he wasn't sure that was how Cassie viewed the situation.

Jordan nodded, then turned his attention back to her. "Are you still taking classes at FCCJ?"

Cassie shook her head and proceeded to tell him about taking in her sister's children. Soon they were engaged in an animated conversation, and Jordan introduced her to several other people. Wade was left at the edge of the group, who helped themselves to the hors d'oeuvres being passed around the ballroom. He took an hors d'oeuvre and stood there munching on it while he tried to figure out how to recapture his date without being overbearing.

Angie appeared at his side. "Where's Cassie?"

Wade nodded toward the group, where Cassie was now the center of attention. "Right over there."

Angie chuckled. "And she was so worried about not fitting in. Look at her shine."

"Yeah, it's great, isn't it?" Wade hoped he sounded sincere.

"Thanks for being such a good escort for her. You haven't monopolized her time. You've allowed her to spread her wings. Now she's gained some confidence." Angie laid a hand on his arm. "Maybe I shouldn't say this, but you should know she was very nervous about this evening, mainly because she wanted to impress you. So I'm glad it's going well."

"Me, too," Wade said, surprised at Angie's comment.

He would never have guessed Cassie was out to impress him. Where had Angie come up with that idea? From all of Wade's observations, Cassie had seemed more comfortable with Jordan and his friends. Maybe that was for the best. She was a beautiful young woman with her whole life in front of her. What did she need with a guy his age, who came with the burden of a bad health history?

Chapter Thirteen

Cassie searched the room for Wade. He stood nearby, talking with a group of men. This evening wasn't turning out as she'd hoped. So much for impressing the one man she wanted to impress. As soon as Jordan introduced himself, Wade had made himself scarce, seemingly eager to step away. Angie's assessment of Wade's interest in her was obviously wrong. He seemed uptight, or perhaps annoyed that he'd had to bring her to this event. He was probably afraid she would embarrass him by saying the wrong thing or using the wrong fork at dinner.

Well, she wasn't going to give up on impressing Wade. Seeing Jordan again served to remind her of the life she'd left behind. He was a handsome young guy, closer to her age, but he held no attraction for her. During their conversation, she'd discovered that his interests still centered on the party scene. That wasn't what she wanted out of life. She'd seen where that road could lead. She wanted a man whose life centered on God. That man was Wade Dalton. But how was she going to capture his attention?

When dinner was finally announced, all the guests made their way to the tables. Sitting next to Wade, Cassie was thankful for the assigned seats. Now that he was more or less captive beside her, could she dazzle him with scintillating conversation? Or would he look at her through the eyes of a man who had chased her around the beach while he squirted her with a water launcher? What chance was there to make him think of her as sophisticated and charming if *that* image was stuck in his mind? She tried to push those questions away while the pastor of one of the local churches gave a blessing for the food.

After the blessing, the servers brought out the salad. Cassie watched others at the table to make sure she used the right fork. She talked with the couple sitting next to her as she tried to remember to ask questions to show an interest in them. She learned that the couple was involved in the local book festival, held every year on the island in early October.

"I hope you'll try to attend," the woman said.

"I'm caring for my sister's children right now, so they keep me pretty busy," Cassie said, hoping she wouldn't have to explain the circumstances.

"Oh, they have a wonderful program for the children on Saturday. You'll have to bring them. I know they would enjoy it so much."

"That seems like such a long ways away."

The woman chuckled. "Yes, but not for those of us who are working to put it all together. It takes a lot of time and volunteers."

Soon the servers whisked away the empty salad plates and presented the main course. During the meal,

Cassie realized the people sitting around her were mostly wealthy retirees who gladly gave of their time and money to make the community a better place. She was completely amazed that, as the recipient of the kind of charities they supported, she was rubbing elbows with the well-to-do. Even though Wade talked more with the people next to him than with her, she didn't feel out of place, as she had when they first arrived.

When the servers brought around the dessert, Wade leaned over and whispered, "You seem to be having a good time."

"I am."

"That's good to hear." He winked at her. "Seems that you're a hit with young and old alike."

"I guess." She forced herself to smile, wishing she could be a hit with him. Was he just making sure she was having a good time to please Angie?

After dinner, Angie and another woman presented some information about the mentoring program and the many volunteers who worked to help youngsters succeed. Cassie wondered whether Wade was thinking that she was one of those who had been helped by this program. She was grateful for the help she'd received, but it always made her feel a little inferior.

Then one of the other sponsors introduced the speaker for the evening. A man who looked to be in his fifties, with salt-and-pepper hair, walked to the podium. He entertained the crowd with a humorous yet inspirational talk that included snippets of his life and how a mentoring program had saved him from a life of crime and helped him become a successful businessman.

By the end of his talk, Cassie realized that she

shouldn't be ashamed or feel inferior. She should be willing to show others what the mentoring program meant to her. So when he asked those in the audience who had been helped by a mentor to stand, Cassie stood, blinking back tears as the audience applauded. She glanced around the room and saw how many others were standing.

When the applause dwindled, she glanced at Wade. He gazed up at her, and she read the admiration in his eyes as he adjusted his glasses. Her heart jumped into her throat, and her pulse raced as she returned to her seat. After she sat down, she received congratulations from everyone at the table, but nothing could top the way Wade's appreciation made her feel.

The event drew to a close, and many of the attendees came up to Cassie and congratulated her and wished her well. Wade hovered nearby, still wearing that admiring smile. She felt as though her heart were soaring around the room. This night had begun to exceed all her expectations. Was her fairy-tale dream coming true?

As folks started to leave, Wade put his hand to her back and escorted her to the door. She couldn't ignore the way his touch sent little sparks through her midsection, but she had to keep herself from just leaning into him or throwing her arms around his neck. She feared she might do just that when they were alone.

Just before they stepped into the hallway outside the ballroom, Angie rushed over and gave Cassie a hug, then held her at arm's length. "I'm so proud of you." Then Angie glanced at Wade. "She was the most beautiful woman here, wasn't she?"

Nodding, Wade smiled. "My thoughts exactly."

Cassie felt the heat rise in her cheeks. They were probably the same color as her dress. "Okay, you two, you're embarrassing me now."

"You're too modest," Angie said with a wave of her hand. "I just wanted to let you know I'm going out of town next week to a Realtors' symposium in Colorado. I'm a little concerned about the hurricane that's sitting out there. It may interfere with my return trip."

Cassie wrinkled her brow. "How?"

"If it comes anywhere close to Jacksonville, they'll close the airport, and I won't be able to get back home." Angie sighed. "Do you have a plan if you have to evacuate?"

Shaking her head, Cassie worried her lower lip. "I guess I'll have to go to a shelter."

"You need to have a plan in place. If you have to evacuate, I'll call and give you instructions about the hurricane shutters and turning off all the utilities." Angie patted Cassie's shoulder. "I don't mean to worry you, but we have to be prepared."

"I can help her, because I'll have to do all the same things with my place, and she can go with me to my parents' house in Atlanta if we have to evacuate," Wade said.

"I couldn't ask your parents to take me in, and four little kids, too." Cassie glanced at Angie. "Besides, what would the caseworker say?"

Angie patted Cassie's arm. "I'm sure she'll okay your evacuation plans. After all, everything went well when she visited."

"That was a big relief for us all," Cassie said.

Wade stared at her with concern. "Cassie, I wouldn't

feel right letting you and the kids go to a shelter while I go to my parents' place."

"Well, I'll let you two battle this out. I've got to be on my way. Let's just hope the hurricane stays away. Then we won't have to worry about any of it."

"That's what we can pray for." Cassie gave Angie another hug before she hurried away.

Wade moved into the hallway. "Let's head home."

They rode back to the town houses in silence. Cassie wondered what Wade was thinking. Despite his compliments and admiring looks at the end of the evening, she still wasn't sure how he viewed her. Maybe all that had nothing to do with his thoughts about her as a woman. He could still be looking at her as nothing more than the nice young woman next door who had managed to overcome her rotten upbringing with the help of a fine lady like Angie.

After he pulled his SUV into the garage, he turned and looked at her. "It's a nice evening, and still early. Would you like to take a little walk?"

When she realized he wasn't eager for their evening to end, her pulse seemed to be hammering all over her body. She swallowed a big lump in her throat. "Sure."

She started to open the door, but he rushed around to her side and opened it for her. He took hold of her hand. "Let me help you."

The warmth and strength of his hand, wrapped around hers, created a deep longing in her soul. Pressure built in her chest as he gazed at her. Did his attention mean what she hoped it did? She took in a shaky breath, and when she spoke, her voice came out in barely a whisper. "Sure."

Oh, man, was that all she could say? Her brain was mush.

Obviously not caring about her one-word vocabulary, he smiled at her and continued to hold her hand as they walked out of the garage. She felt as though she were floating while he led her toward the walk that went between the two buildings and connected with the dunes walkover. The warm breeze rustled the sea oats on the dunes and made the hem of her dress flutter around her legs. Her heart beat in the same fluttery rhythm.

They climbed the steps of the walkover and strolled to the end, where the moonlight illuminated the waves breaking on the beach. Stars sprinkled the darkened sky with pinpricks of light. The peaceful night belied the hurricane looming in distant waters, yet a hurricane of emotions brewed inside Cassie as Wade put an arm around her shoulders and pulled her close.

As they stood side by side, they didn't speak, as if talking would somehow ruin the moment. Drinking in the security of having Wade's arm around her, she sighed.

"Why the sigh?" He gave her shoulders a squeeze and turned her to face him.

Swallowing a lump in her throat, she looked up at him. Her stomach did that little flip-flop. "Contentment. Thank you for taking me to dinner. I enjoyed it more than I ever imagined."

He pulled her closer, and she put her arms around his waist. "It was my pleasure to take you. I should be the one thanking you for the privilege of escorting the most beautiful woman there."

Heat rose in her cheeks. His compliment meant more now, because he'd had no prompting from Angie or other bystanders. Looking up at him, she said, "You're making me blush again."

"You're cute when you blush, but it's too dark to see now," he said with a lopsided grin.

"Are you making fun of me?"

"Absolutely not. There's only one thing I'm thinking about right now." He caressed her cheek with the back of his index finger. Then he tilted her face up to his, and she knew he was going to kiss her. Every nerve in her body was wired as their lips met.

She felt like a fairy-tale princess, and Wade was definitely her handsome prince. When the kiss ended, she stood in the circle of his arms and wished the moment would never end. They stood quietly for a few moments while the waves rushing onto the beach sounded through the night air.

"I've been wanting to do that for weeks."

His statement emboldened her. "What took you so long?"

Laughing, he held her at arm's length. "Do I have to admit I thought you surely couldn't be interested in the old guy next door?"

"Only if you want."

"I think I just did." He laughed again. "You know, Cassie, these past few weeks have brought me more fun than I've have had in a long, long time. You and the kids have brightened my life."

"And you've done the same for us." She blinked back threatening tears.

"But it's more than that." He pulled her into the circle of his arms again. "I've watched you with the kids and grown to admire so much about you. And little by little

I found myself caring more and more about you, but I pushed away those feelings."

"Why?"

"I didn't think I was the right man for you, because of our age difference. Seeing you with that young guy tonight had me convinced I was right, even after Angie told me you wanted to impress me tonight."

"She did?"

"Yeah. Thanks to Angie for a little matchmaking, I just couldn't get her statement out of my mind and decided to do something about it. Like tell you how much I care about you."

"And I care about you, too. Seeing Jordan tonight made that clear. You're a much better man. The kind of man I want in my life."

When she looked up, he leaned over and kissed her again. His lips lingered, and she wrapped her arms around his neck. He held her tight. The starry sky, the warm gentle breeze, the peaceful sounds of the surf and the breathtaking kisses from the most incredible man made this a perfect night. Dreams *did* come true.

Dark clouds roiled overhead, and a big gust of wind nearly slammed the door on one of Wade's legs as he slid behind the steering wheel of his SUV. He glanced back at the kids, who were buckled into their seats and sleeping soundly.

He reached across the console and squeezed Cassie's hand. "Ready?"

Nodding, she tried to smile, but he read the worry in her eyes. "I think so. I hope we remembered to do everything."

"Between the two of us, I'm sure we've done what we can to protect the town houses from the storm. And we'll be taking what's most important with us." He glanced at the sleeping children in the back. "There's nothing more we can do now except pray that it doesn't hit too hard."

"Are you sure your parents are ready for this crew?"

Wade chuckled. "You don't have to worry about my parents."

"But I do. This has to be a terrible inconvenience for them."

"Cassie, haven't you learned over the past two weeks that I love you and the kids? So will my parents."

"I wish I were as confident as you are."

"No need to worry."

"If you say so."

"I do." He started the engine and backed out of the drive. "We're on our way. If you're tired, I don't care if you want to go to sleep."

"Right now I'm too keyed up to sleep. Besides, I want to keep you company."

"Okay."

The headlights beamed into the predawn and illuminated the Spanish moss swaying with the gusts of wind that blew through the branches of the live oaks lining the road. Even though they were leaving at four-thirty in the morning, a line of other vehicles stretched out ahead of them when Wade drove across the Shave Bridge connecting Amelia Island with the mainland.

As he lost the view of the island in his rearview mirror, he prayed that the storm would pass them by and leave the beauty of the barrier island untouched. The weather forecast predicted landfall within the next twenty-four hours for the hurricane spinning off the Florida coastline. It had meandered around the Caribbean for a week before finally making a move north. The past two weeks had brought Cassie and him closer, but this had been an anxiety-filled time. They watched the storm strike several Caribbean islands and lose strength, only to regain it as it passed over open water. Now it appeared to be headed their way.

Traffic continued to be heavy on I-95, but it became lighter when Wade turned onto I-16 and headed for Macon, Georgia. Wade glanced over at Cassie. Her head bobbed forward. Then she jerked awake.

With a sheepish grin, she turned and looked at him. "Guess I'm not so wide awake as I thought."

"If you're sleepy, take a nap. I'll be fine. I promise, if I get tired I'll pull over. We'll stop for breakfast when the kids are awake."

"I think I'll take a little nap." She grabbed a pillow from the backseat and laid her head against it.

In minutes, she appeared to have joined the kids in sleep. Miles later the sky lightened, as they drove away from the cloud cover from the brewing storm. Wade continued to drive and glanced occasionally at Cassie who slept so peacefully.

The beauty of her spirit only enhanced her physical beauty. The night of the charity dinner had changed everything about their relationship. Wade wondered whether the kids recognized a difference. Or were they oblivious to the sparks crackling between the two adults? He'd halfway expected Makayla to pick up on their newfound relationship, but so far she hadn't suggested again that he and Cassie get married.

Cassie made him feel more alive than he had in years, but that reminded him of the one thing marring their relationship. He'd never told her about his battle with Hodgkin's disease. He had to tell her, but he feared her reaction.

He was in love. With Cassie. With these four little kids. He owed it to them to be upfront about his past health issues. Even though he'd tried to bring it up several times over the past two weeks, he'd chickened out every time. The words had sat on the tip of his tongue while they were at the beach, while they played at the pool and while they gazed into each other's eyes. But he couldn't say them. He couldn't face the loss of another woman he loved because she couldn't deal with the dreaded word *cancer.* Besides, wasn't he cancer-free? The cancer might never return. It might never become an issue. He tried to rationalize with himself, but it didn't make him feel better. He pushed the subject to the back of his mind and decided not to think about it for the rest of the trip.

By the time Wade parked his SUV in front of the red-brick one-and-a-half-story house that had been his boyhood home, the kids were antsy from the long ride. He glanced back at them. "We're here."

"Can we get out now?" Makayla asked, already unbuckling her seat belt.

Cassie turned and held out a cautioning hand as Taylor and Jack unbuckled their seat belts, as well. "Just hold on until Mr. Wade tells us where to go."

Looking at Cassie, Wade opened his door and got out. "They can get out. When I talked to my mom, she said to make ourselves at home. She and Dad will be home in a couple of hours, around four o'clock."

"Okay, kids, everybody out." Cassie unbuckled Danny and picked him up while the other children scrambled from the car.

"This is a cool place," Makayla said as she ran around the neatly manicured yard.

"Well, if you think this is cool, follow me." Wade led them around the back of the house into a fenced back-yard containing a wooden swing set with a slide and jungle gym.

While the older children ran to play, Wade led Cassie to a screened-in porch at the back of the house. "We can sit here for a while."

"Okay." Still holding Danny, she sat on one of the wicker chairs surrounding a round wicker table.

After flipping on the ceiling fan in the porch, Wade unlocked the back door and went inside. He returned with a pitcher of lemonade and some paper cups. He served everyone, then joined Cassie at the table while the kids ran back to play. Despite the heat of a humid July afternoon, the shade of the old oak and maple trees kept the backyard cool.

While the children played and Cassie relaxed on the porch, Wade unloaded the necessary luggage and brought it into the house. He took his things to his old room, where he'd stayed during his treatment for Hodgkin's disease. Being there reminded him that he still hadn't told Cassie. How was he going to approach the subject?

His gaze fell on the Bible sitting on the nightstand. He should pray about it, but did he really want to know God's purpose? Or was he just trying to figure this out on his own? He left the room without answering the question or calling on God for help. He didn't want to be disappointed again. He'd been pushing God farther and farther away from this decision.

When he returned to the porch, he found Cassie still holding Danny. Anxiety appeared to have etched little furrows between Cassie's eyebrows.

"Are you okay?" he asked her.

"Yeah. I was just wondering whether you got everything unloaded?"

"I did." He sat down beside her, not fooled by her forced smile, and patted her hand. "Now tell me what's really troubling you."

She released a harsh breath. "I'm just worried about meeting your folks." She looked up at the ceiling, then back at him. "Oh, I hope the kids behave."

"Quit worrying. How could my parents not love you? I do." He chuckled. "They raised three rambunctious boys. They know how children are."

Cassie's eyes opened wide. "I've never thought of you as a kid."

"You mean you think I was born old?"

"Yes, sir." She laughed.

He joined in her laughter. But the levity didn't linger in his heart, because of an important confession that he couldn't bring himself to make.

At four o'clock on the dot, Cassie heard the door from the kitchen open onto the porch. She glanced up, and her heart began to pound as an elegant, dark-haired woman in a beige pantsuit stepped through the door.

"Hello. You must be Cassie." Smiling, the woman extended her hand.

"Yes, and this is Danny." Cassie glanced at the happy

toddler in her arms as she jumped up from her seat and shook the woman's hand.

"Welcome. I'm Gloria Dalton." She turned to the tall, gray-haired man who followed her through the door. "And this is my husband, Harold."

Cassie shook his hand as Wade, who had been playing in the yard with the older kids, loped to the back porch. The kids followed, and he herded them to a stop in front of his parents. He gave his mom a quick hug, and shook hands with his dad. Then he introduced the kids. Cassie breathed a mental sigh of relief when they very politely said hello, and she had to stifle a giggle when Jack shook hands with Wade's dad as Wade had done.

After the introductions, the children ran back into the yard to play—even Danny, who toddled along with Taylor. Wade served more lemonade as his parents joined Cassie at the table. "Mom, I didn't know where you wanted Cassie and the kids to sleep, so I left their things in the front hallway."

"We'll have to figure that out after your brother Peter gets here." Raising her hands, Gloria clasped them together. "He called about half an hour ago, and said he'd be over for dinner."

Wade smiled. "That's great."

Gloria stood. "I'd better get things going in the kitchen."

"Can I help?" Cassie hopped up.

Heading inside, Gloria smiled. "Certainly, dear. That'll give us a chance to chat without the men."

"I'll just get Danny before I come in."

Wade grabbed her arm as she started for the back-yard. "You go ahead with Mom. I'll get him."

"Okay," Cassie said, feeling as though Wade was trying very hard to show his family that he cared about her kids. What did his parents think? She hoped they approved. So far, they seemed very accepting.

Cassie stepped into the kitchen. Everything gleamed, from the earth-toned granite countertops to the sparkling white appliances and the oak cupboards. "Your kitchen's beautiful."

"Thank you. We've renovated the whole house in the last couple of years. New kitchen. New baths. Feels like a brand-new house, almost." Gloria checked something in the built-in oven, then turned back to Cassie. "I'm cooking Wade's favorite—pot roast with potatoes and carrots. I was able to run home between classes earlier today and put it in the oven."

"Smells good," Cassie said, wishing she'd known before now that Wade liked pot roast.

"All we have to do besides set the table is make a salad and cook the green beans. They're fresh from our neighbor's garden." Gloria got a salad bowl and a saucepan out of the cupboard and got a bag of beans and the fixings for a salad out of the refrigerator. Then she turned to Cassie. "Before we do this, let's figure out where you're going to sleep."

"I really hate putting you out like this, but Wade insisted we come with him."

"And he was right to do that. I can't imagine having to go to a shelter, especially with the children. We have plenty of room."

Following Gloria through the house, Cassie took in the shiny hardwood floors and the oriental rugs that coordinated so well with the furnishings. Every room looked like something out of a decorator's magazine.

Each piece of bric-a-brac filled the perfect spot. There wasn't a speck of dirt or dust in sight.

Her heart plummeted when she thought of the children in this house. She feared the worst. How was she going to keep them from breaking something? It was hard to believe three boys had grown up in this house. Maybe everything hadn't been so perfect before the recent renovations Gloria had mentioned. No matter. They were here, and the children would have to deal with this, hopefully for only a few days.

Gloria showed her a room with twin beds decorated with matching striped comforters in soft greens and golds. "You can have this room. Did you want the children to stay with you?"

"I brought a portable crib for Danny that I can put up in here." Cassie gestured toward the bed. "The other children can share the bed."

"Oh, I didn't mean they should all share this one bed. I have inflatable beds to put in here, if that's where the children would feel more comfortable, or I can put them in the rec room downstairs."

"I'll keep the boys with me, but the girls might like the rec room. I'll ask them."

"Wonderful." Gloria stepped into the hallway. "If you don't mind, you could start making the salad while I go change into something more comfortable."

"Sure," Cassie said, glad that Wade's mom wasn't treating her like some pampered guest.

Going back to the kitchen, Cassie passed a sunny room at the front of the house with a wall of bookcases filled with books and trophies. A mahogany desk and a warm-brown leather sofa completed the room. Wade would look right at home in this room. But the room, and the rest of the house, reminded Cassie that she and Wade had grown up in two different worlds. Over the past couple of weeks, she had almost forgotten. And Wade had never made it an issue, so why should she?

While Cassie was putting a variety of greens in the salad bowl, Gloria returned, dressed in a pair of navy capri pants, a coordinating print top and a pair of sandals.

Gloria picked up the bag of beans and took them to the sink. "Now I'm more comfortable. Looks like you've got a good start on the salad."

"Yes, ma'am."

"Have you heard anything more about the hurricane?"

"Not since we left."

"Let's see what we can find out." Gloria turned on a small TV that sat on the kitchen counter and located a station that was giving an update on the storm.

Just as they started to listen, Wade and his dad, along with the children and another man, who had to be Wade's brother, bustled into the kitchen. The two brothers had the same color hair and eyes, but Peter was a couple of inches taller.

"Peter, you're here." Gloria crossed the room and hugged her other son.

"Yeah, I found Dad and Wade playing tag with these kids." Grinning, Peter reached down and tapped them each on the head.

"Aunt Cassie, this is Mr. Peter, he's Mr. Wade's brother," Makayla announced. "He told me and Taylor we're pretty."

Peter stepped forward and shook Cassie's hand. "Looks like they take after their aunt."

Cassie blushed. "Thank you. Nice to meet you."

Wade looked at the TV. "What's the news on the hurricane?"

Gloria turned up the volume. "I don't know. We missed it when you came in."

For a few minutes, everyone's attention was focused on the report coming from the small screen. While they watched, Wade stood behind Cassie and put his hands on her shoulders.

"Wow! A category three." Harold glanced over his shoulder at Wade. "Look at that thing spinning away in the Atlantic."

"Good news, though. It's not going to make landfall in our area," Wade said. "It's just going to sideswipe the island. That'll limit the damage."

"We'll pray that's the case." Gloria shut off the TV. "When will you be able to go back?"

"My friend Angie's going to call to let us know."

"I'll get a call from work, too," Wade said.

"And we'll monitor the situation as well as we can from here." Harold looked at the kids. "Who wants to help me set the table?"

Taylor, Makayla and Jack immediately volunteered. Cassie watched Wade's dad lead the merry parade into the dining room. Wade may not have been around children much, but Cassie knew where he'd learned his skills with children.

While Gloria and Cassie put the finishing touches on dinner, Wade and Peter played a little one-on-one basketball using the hoop in the backyard. Dicing tomatoes for the salad, Cassie viewed the competition through the kitchen window as she talked with Gloria. After everyone went into the dining room for dinner, despite the fact that Wade's parents had welcomed Cassie and the children with open arms, she knew all of Gloria's very tactful questions were an attempt to find out everything she could about the woman her son had brought home. What did Wade's family really think about his attachment to her and the kids?

Chapter Fourteen

"Wade, what are your intentions toward that girl?"

Wade glanced up to see his mother standing just inside the doorway to his bedroom. "Intentions?"

"There's no disguising that you think you're in love with her." His mother eyed him. "Are you planning to marry her?"

"What if I am?"

Gloria stepped further into the room. "You deserve better than a ready-made family."

"And she deserves better than a man with a bad medical history. I'm grateful she cares about me."

"Is that what this is all about? You think no one can love you because you've had cancer?"

"Julia didn't stick around."

"So you're going to jump right into this relationship without really thinking it through?"

"What makes you think I haven't done that?" Wade glared at his mother. "I thought you liked her and the kids."

"I do. She's quite lovely, but she's not for you. You've

known her what—two months at the most? How can you know your feelings are for real after so little time?"

Wade let out a harsh laugh. "You think time makes a difference? I dated Julia for two years, and we were engaged for one. Little good that did."

"Okay." Gloria waved a hand, as if to dismiss his argument. "So you believe you're in love. Are you ready to take on the responsibility for someone else's children?"

"She has, and I want to be a part of that."

"That's what you think now, because you're taken in by a pretty face."

"She's not just a pretty face, Mom. She's energetic, loving, caring. I can't begin to describe all her wonderful attributes."

"That's all well and good, but she doesn't even have a college education. You've always been around educated people."

"I can't believe I'm hearing you say this. Have you become some sort of academic snob? You can't associate with people who aren't as educated as you? Not all learning comes from books and college courses. Life can teach you lessons you can't get anywhere else. Battling cancer taught me a lot about life and who I am. And Cassie has taught me about love. Real love."

Wade's mother shook her head. "I didn't mean it that way."

"Then what did you mean?"

Gloria didn't say anything for a few moments. Finally, she patted Wade on the arm. "I just want you to really think this relationship over. You're a well-educated and brilliant man. Will this young woman fulfill your needs on an intellectual level?"

"This is ridiculous—"

"Just hear me out." Gloria gave him a stern look. "You might think it's not a problem, but years down the road things may be different. And the kids. You've been a bachelor, living on your own, for years. Are you ready, day in and day out, for a houseful of children? And they've come from a terrible background. Don't you think that'll affect them later on? What will happen when they're teenagers? It's hard enough to rear children that are your own, much less someone else's."

"Where's your Christian charity? These kids deserve a family as much as anyone."

"Don't think about marrying this girl out of charity."

"You think this is all about charity? Not charity, Mom. Love." Wade paused for a moment. "Come to think about it, the word *charity* is used in the King James Version of the Bible in place of *love.* 'Though I speak with the tongues of men and of angels, and have not charity, I am become as sounding brass, or a tinkling cymbal.' I don't want to be sounding brass, just talking about love but never showing it."

"I still think you're making a mistake in pursuing this relationship. She may be a wonderful girl, but she's not right for you." Gloria stared at him. "Does she know about the cancer?"

Wade gazed at the floor. He couldn't look his mother in the eye.

"You haven't told her, have you?"

Looking up, he grimaced. "No."

"Then what makes you think she'll be any different than Julia?"

"I just know."

"Well then, you'd better tell her—or I will."

"I don't want to discuss this anymore." Wade shook his head. "We're never going to agree about this." Wade turned to leave and caught sight of Cassie retreating down the hall. What had she heard?

He chased after her. "Cassie, wait!"

"Leave me alone, Wade."

"Let me explain."

"What's to explain? Your mother doesn't think I'm good enough for you. And you must feel the same way. You never told me about the cancer."

Wade felt like he was dying inside. Why *hadn't* he told her? "Please listen. My Hodgkin's disease is in remission."

"I'm glad that's the case, but it still doesn't change the fact that you didn't tell me."

"I couldn't talk about it in front of the children, and every time I tried to bring it up, I was afraid. Afraid you wouldn't love me."

"Then you don't know me very well, do you?"

"I was wrong. I should've trusted you with the information."

"Well, I know now, and it doesn't make any difference to me. But the fact that you didn't tell me does. I heard you tell your mother that I taught you about love. Well, I must've done a terrible job, because you didn't love me enough to share your troubles with me. You didn't trust *my* love enough."

"That's not true."

"You might say the words, but your actions tell me something different." Cassie put her fingers to her temples. "I came to tell you Angie called. We can go back to the island. She says the town houses have water damage from the storm surge and wind damage to the roofs."

"Then you can't go back. You won't be able to stay there."

"Angie said the kids and I can stay with her until the repairs are done."

"But won't there be a problem finding someone to do the work?"

Cassie smiled for the first time since their discussion had begun. "Angie's first in line, because she's the boss of her own construction company."

"I forgot about that."

"You won't be able to live in your place, either. What will you do?"

"I'll be on the road. I'll be doing a lot of field assessment. Downed trees. Road repair. After I assess the damage, I'll have to determine if salvage crews need to be brought in to harvest the damaged timber. So I won't be home."

"That'll be best. We won't have to see each other." Cassie turned to go, then stopped. "I'll be ready to go as soon as we're packed. I don't want to burden your parents or you any longer."

Cassie walked back into the town house with the children. Everything seemed the same as it had been before the hurricane, except that the smell of newly laid carpet filled the air. Returning to the town house reminded her of Wade and the tense ride home from Atlanta three weeks ago. Thankfully, the children hadn't recognized the friction between her and Wade. With a strained goodbye, he'd dropped her off at Angie's. That was the last she'd seen or heard from him. Had he already moved back in to his town house next door, or had he found another place to live?

Makayla tugged on Cassie's arm. "Is Mr. Wade home? Can we go see him?"

"He's probably working."

"But, Aunt Cassie, this is a Saturday, and Mr. Wade doesn't work on Saturdays."

"Normally that's true, but he's probably been working this Saturday, because they're still doing clean-up from the hurricane. He'll be way too busy to see us." Cassie set Danny on the couch. "Taylor, will you keep an eye on him while I bring in the suitcases?"

"Yes, ma'am."

While Cassie unloaded the car, her mind was a jumble of troubling thoughts about Wade. The summer was nearly over. School would start in a week. With school to occupy Makayla's mind, maybe she wouldn't ask every day about Wade. Hopefully, the kids would soon forget him. That was what she was hoping for herself, but he was constantly on her mind. Even the busy weeks at the insurance agency hadn't helped her forget. She longed to see his smiling face and hear his voice, but what would be the point?

Her initial anger over his reluctance to tell her about his bout with cancer had subsided, but that wasn't the real issue, anyway. Despite Wade's pleas to the contrary, his mother was right. Wade needed someone from his world—someone who could be an asset to him, rather than a burden.

His mother's objection to their relationship had come as such a surprise. The woman had been so welcoming.

She'd taken Cassie garage-sale hopping and bought the kids lots of wonderful, inexpensive clothes. She'd told Cassie she used to shop at garage sales all the time when her boys were little, but now Cassie wondered whether the woman had thought it was something that would appeal to Cassie because of her upbringing. And why had Gloria introduced her to everyone at their church as Wade's girlfriend? Maybe she'd figured those people would never see Cassie again.

But the biggest puzzle of all was the way she'd treated the children. She'd played games with them and sat and read stories to them. She'd even helped to tuck them in at night. Then she'd said all those awful things. Nearly a month later, Cassie still couldn't get the hurtful words out of her mind. Her heart ached for the children, because they loved Wade so much, but then, so did she. Their relationship could never work, because his mother was so vehemently opposed to it.

Trying to put him out of her mind, she went to the car to bring in the last of the suitcases. She hoped he had found another place to live.

"Aunt Cassie, I saw Mr. Wade." Makayla raced in from the patio, leaving the door wide open. "He's coming back from the beach. I want to see him."

"No." Cassie went to close the door and caught a glimpse of Wade as he walked toward his town house. Her heart fluttered when she saw him wearing his Indiana Jones hat. Steeling herself against the reaction, she immediately turned and marched across the room and plucked Danny off the couch.

"Why not?"

"Because you have to help put away your things.

When that's done, maybe you can go see him." Cassie didn't know how she was going to deal with seeing Wade again, but putting it off for a while was the best she could do for now. "Now, get moving."

The girls and Jack charged ahead as they dragged their new school backpacks up the stairs to their rooms. Following close behind, Cassie carried Danny and one of the suitcases. When she reached the top of the stairs, she set Danny down. He scrambled to catch up to Jack, who stopped for a moment in the doorway to his bedroom. When Danny drew close, Jack darted into the room and tried to close the door. Danny screamed. Dropping the suitcase, Cassie raced to see what had happened.

She reached down to pick him up. One of his little fingers was caught in the door. Pushing on the door, she immediately extracted his finger. Blood dripped everywhere as she raced to the bathroom. His screams continued to pierce the air as she turned on the water and held his hand under the faucet to wash away the blood. When she looked down at the finger and saw the damage, her head spun and her knees grew weak. She steadied herself against the counter. Breathing deeply, she grabbed a nearby towel and wrapped it around the bloody finger. *Think. Don't go to pieces.* There was only one thing to do. She had to take Danny to the emergency room.

She scrambled down the stairs. Taylor and Makayla were right behind her. Her heart hammering, she looked for her purse and keys and spied them on the kitchen table.

"Aunt Cassie, what's wrong with Danny?" Makayla's high-pitched little voice made Cassie look down.

With Danny's cries still ringing in her ears, Cassie

stared down at the two little girls, who looked up at her with wide, worried eyes. She put her free hand to her forehead. What was she going to do with the other kids while she went to the hospital? How could she drive and take care of Danny at the same time?

Finally, pushing away her panic, she answered, "He hurt his finger."

Makayla ran for the door. "I'll get Mr. Wade to help."

"Yes. Get Mr. Wade."

Wade sat in the emergency room, the drone of a TV program serving as background noise for the hustle and bustle around him. Despite Danny's continued cries, he would be okay. But Wade wondered whether his own heart was going to be okay now that he'd seen Cassie again.

"Mr. Wade, what are they doing to Danny?" Taylor looked at him, concern painted across her face.

"The doctor's going to fix his finger by putting some stitches in it."

"What are stitches?" Makayla asked.

Wade wondered whether he could explain the procedure to a five-year-old. "When someone gets a bad cut, the doctor sews it closed with stitches."

"Does it hurt?" Makayla wrinkled her little nose.

"A little, but it'll make Danny's finger all better. Don't worry. He'll be fine."

"Is Jack in trouble?" Makayla asked.

Wade glanced down at the little boy sitting on his lap. "No, it was an accident, but you all have to be more careful when you close the doors."

As Wade talked with the kids about safety, a woman approached him. "Are you Wade Dalton?"

"Yes, why?"

"Ms. Rankin asked me to let you know the little boy who came in with her will have to wait for treatment because we've received an accident victim in a life-threatening situation." The woman motioned toward the area on the other side of the waiting room. "But they're waiting comfortably in one of the rooms."

"Thanks for letting me know," Wade replied.

"Where's Aunt Cassie and Danny?" Taylor worried her bottom lip as she looked up at him.

"They're waiting for the doctor. The lady just said it'll be a little while longer."

Taylor gripped one of Wade's arms. "Why do we have to wait longer?"

"Because someone who is much sicker than Danny has come in, and they have to take care of them first."

"How long do we have to wait?" Makayla asked.

"I don't know." Wade said, wondering whether he'd be fielding questions every two minutes. Then he noticed a Bible storybook sitting on a table nearby and reached over and picked it up. "Let's read a story while we're waiting." Wade started to read, and the girls leaned closer to see the pictures.

After he had read several stories, Makayla began to fidget. "Is Danny still going to be okay?"

Wade nodded and patted Makayla's hand. "Yes. Do you want to say a prayer for him?"

Taylor nodded. "Can we pray for the other person, too?"

"Yes, we should do that." Putting his arms around the girls and Jack, Wade gathered them all close.

He said a short prayer, and then each of the kids—

even Jack—took turns praying. When they finished, Wade realized what a wonderful job Cassie had done in teaching these little children about trusting in God. Had he been trusting in God the way he should? He thought about the person who lay in a life-and-death situation in a room nearby.

Then it hit him. No one knew when such circumstances might come into his life. Young or old, healthy or unhealthy. He'd been living his life letting fear of a recurrence of the cancer rob him of the chance to share life with a wonderful woman and four great kids. He had to convince Cassie that they were right for each other. He added that thought to his prayer as he drew the kids close for a hug.

Cassie stopped just outside the waiting room. Wade held Jack on his lap, while Taylor and Makayla sat on either side of him.

"Mr. Wade, I want you to be there to take care of us all the time." Makayla reached up and put her arms around his neck. "I love you."

"Me, too." Taylor joined in the group hug. "I missed you, Mr. Wade. I was sad without you."

"And I was sad without you, too." Wade ruffled Taylor's hair. "It's been too lonely without you."

"I said if we were your kids, you wouldn't be lonely." Self-satisfaction came through in Makayla's every word. "And I liked being at your mom and daddy's house. Can we visit again?"

At that moment, Cassie realized Wade's mother had been wrong. He needed them, and they needed him. Cassie wasn't going to let someone else decide what would make Wade and her and the kids happy. But could he forgive her for pushing him away? Maybe Makayla's plea would go a long way toward convincing him that he had a welcome place in their family.

Wade glanced up, and Cassie's heart skipped a beat. She tried to smile. "Well, we're ready to go home."

Wade jumped up. "How's the patient?"

"Okay." Cassie showed off his bandaged finger. "All stitched up."

"Good. Let's head home." Wade fished his keys from his pants pocket.

"Sure." Cassie followed him and the kids to the car and wondered what he could be thinking.

She sat in the backseat with Danny and stared at the back of Wade's head on the ride home. He didn't say much, other than to field a few questions from Makayla about what he'd been doing since they'd come back from Atlanta. He was friendly with the kids, polite but distant with her.

She was determined to find a way to talk with him and prayed that God would give her the opportunity and help her say the right things. She wanted to repair her relationship with Wade, but in the end, she had to leave it all in God's hands.

When they arrived back at the town houses, Wade stopped his SUV in her driveway. Her stomach took a nosedive when he turned and looked at her. "Would you like me to take the older kids for ice cream while you get Danny settled? I think they deserve a reward for being so good at the hospital."

Makayla clapped her hands. "Aunt Cassie, please let us go."

Cassie wanted to laugh and cheer, because Wade wanted to take the kids, or he wouldn't have asked in front of them. But he looked so serious that she didn't dare. "Thanks. That would be very helpful."

But she had second thoughts about his motives when he barely said two words to her as he helped her unlock the door and then left immediately. Maybe he just didn't want to have to deal with her. But she wouldn't let his attitude deter her from her mission to win him back.

As soon as Wade left, Cassie dialed Angie's number. When she answered, Cassie asked, "Is there any chance you can come over?"

Angie laughed. "I'm already on my way. I just finished a showing and was coming over to see how you're doing. I'm just getting off I-95."

"Then you should be here in about twenty minutes."

"Probably. Why?"

"I want you to watch the kids," Cassie said, then told Angie about Danny's accident and the whole situation with Wade.

"I'll do whatever I can to get you two back together again. I've been praying about this ever since you came back."

"Me, too. I was praying that God would help me get over him, but I realized that was the wrong prayer."

After Cassie ended the phone call, she rocked Danny to sleep and put him to bed. Then she changed out of her bloodstained clothing and put on the shorts and top she had recently purchased. She brushed her hair and examined her reflection in the mirror. She wanted to look her best for Wade, but she knew that what she looked like wasn't the important thing. It was what she had to say that would make the difference.

Wade swallowed hard when Cassie stepped out the front door and ushered the children inside where he saw Angie. She waved and closed the door, leaving Cassie and him alone.

"I'd like to talk to you. Will you take a walk with me on the beach?" Without waiting for his answer, she removed her sandals and started down the walk that passed between the buildings.

Wondering why she didn't wait, he took off his shoes and hurried after her. "I have some things I want to say to you, too."

"I get to go first."

"Okay, ladies first," he said, not sure he wanted to hear what she had to say.

They walked across what was left of the undulating dunes that had once swayed with sea oats. A few lone posts, protruding from the sand, were all that remained of the walkover. The storm had destroyed the beauty of the dunes. Wade couldn't help but think that the storm had not only ruined the dunes, but had set up the circumstances that had ruined their relationship.

Even though Cassie had been so determined to talk first, she said nothing as they negotiated the drop-off where the huge waves had washed away the beach. What did she want to say? He wished she'd just get it over with.

Finally, when they reached the packed sand near the water's edge, she turned to look at him. She took a deep breath and blurted, "I don't want to alienate you from your family, but I love you and want to be with you, no matter what."

Wade threw back his head and laughed. Then he grabbed her around the waist and lifted her off her feet as he twirled around on the sand. When he set her down, he kissed her, then held her close. "I never expected to hear you say that, but I'm relieved you did. I love you so much. I'm so sorry I didn't tell you about my cancer."

"That doesn't matter. It never mattered. I love you. The kids love you. And we need you."

"And I need you, too. You and the kids have made me happier than I've ever been in my life. And I believe God wants us to be together."

"Even though your mother disapproves?"

Wade held her at arms' length. "That's not true."

Cassie knit her eyebrows in a puzzled frown. "She said I'm all wrong for you. We both heard her."

"Yeah, but she called me a few days after we left and told me she realized she was wrong and asked for my forgiveness. But in the meantime, *I* had decided I'd been right all along and that you deserved someone younger, who didn't have the chance of getting cancer again."

"It doesn't—"

Wade put a finger to her lips. "I know. I learned that today, sitting in the waiting room. When the accident victim came into the emergency room, I realized no matter how healthy a person is, there are no guarantees for tomorrow. We have to make the best of today. I love you and want all my todays to be spent with you. Will you have me?"

"You know I will."

"Then I can tell Makayla I can be her dad?"

Cassie gave him an impish grin and raced toward the dunes. "Yes, *sir*."

Chasing after her, Wade laughed. When he caught her, he kissed her again. "Remember to say that when I ask for breakfast in bed."

"Yes, sir."

They laughed some more while they walked back, arm in arm. As they washed their feet at the shower, which had somehow survived the storm, she smiled at him. Drawing her close again, he gave Cassie one more kiss before they started toward the town houses. His heart soared like the hawk flying high over the dunes.

When they reached the patio, Taylor, Makayla and Jack came scrambling outside. Grinning widely, Angie stood just inside the door as she held Danny.

"Mr. Wade, I saw you kissing Aunt Cassie," Makayla said.

Wade ruffled her hair. "Is that okay with you?"

Wide-eyed, Makayla looked up at him. "Yes. Does that mean you'll be our daddy?"

"Yeah, we get to be a family."

"Yippee!" Makayla jumped up and down, then launched herself at Wade.

Taylor wrapped her little arms around him. "I'm glad, too."

"Me, too." Jack joined in the hug.

"Let me be the first to say congratulations to you two." Angie set Danny on the patio, and he toddled over. "Here's someone else who wants to join in the celebration."

Wade couldn't quit smiling as he picked Danny up. With the other children still clinging to him, Wade pulled Cassie into the circle. Savoring the group hug, he said a silent prayer of thanks that this incredible young woman cared about him and was willing to share his life. Having Cassie's love was more blessing than he'd ever expected. Then there was the added blessing of these four little ones who had barged into his life— and made him happier than he could have imagined.

* * * * *

Dear Reader,

Thanks so much for reading *Four Little Blessings.* I hope Wade and Cassie's story has brought you a blessing. This story shows the difference people can make in the lives of others. We all need people who will lift us up and make us want to be better. I hope you will find a way to encourage someone to have a closer walk with the Lord.

I enjoyed writing this story because it is set near my home and I have always loved the beach. There is nothing like a walk on the beach to remind me of God's wonderful creation.

I love hearing from readers. You can contact me at P.O. Box 16461, Fernandina Beach, Florida 32035 or through my Web site www.merrilleewhren.com.

May God bless you,

Merrillee Whren

QUESTIONS FOR DISCUSSION

1. At the beginning of the story both Wade and Cassie feel an attraction to each other, but they worry that their age difference will pose a problem. Do you believe that age can make a difference in a relationship? Why or why not?

2. Wade's initial attraction to Cassie comes from her physical beauty, but he knows inner beauty counts more. What does he see in Cassie that makes him know she has inner beauty? Read 1 Samuel 16:7 to add to this discussion.

3. Besides the age difference, what other reason does Wade have for not pursuing his interest in Cassie? Is this a legitimate concern? Why or why not?

4. What does Cassie do that surprises Wade? How does she react? Do you think he handles this situation in the correct way? Why or why not? What can you learn from Matthew 7:1-5 and Galatians 6:1-3 regarding this subject?

5. Cassie is concerned about attending church because she fears the children won't behave. She is also concerned about their lack of "church clothes." What does James 2:1-4 say about this subject? What can churches do to make visitors feel more welcome?

6. Cassie is a new Christian, a babe in Christ. What is she doing to help herself grow? What does 1 Peter 2:1-3 say about growing in Christ?

7. New Christians sometimes struggle with old habits. Cassie struggles with a number of things. How does she handle her struggles? Can mature Christians also struggle with things they know are wrong? Read Romans 7:14-20 to help with this discussion.

8. How do Angie and Wade encourage Cassie? What do Romans 12:6-8, Hebrews 3:12-14 and Hebrews 10:24-25 say about encouragement? Why is it important to encourage each other?

9. When Wade comes to the island, he has a plan for his life. What happens to upset this plan? How does he see God's hand in these circumstances? Have there been times in your life when things didn't go as you planned? Could you see God working in your life at that time? Why or why not?

10. What does Wade realize while he is waiting in the emergency room? Why is it more important not to borrow trouble from the future? What do Matthew 6:33-34 and James 4:13-15 say about this subject?

INTRODUCING

Love Inspired

HISTORICAL

A NEW TWO-BOOK SERIES.

Every month, acclaimed
inspirational authors
will bring you engaging stories
rich with romance, adventure
and faith set in a variety
of vivid historical times.

History begins on **February 12**
wherever you buy books.

Steeple
Hill®

www.SteepleHill.com

REQUEST YOUR FREE BOOKS!

2 FREE INSPIRATIONAL NOVELS
PLUS 2
FREE
MYSTERY GIFTS

YES! Please send me 2 FREE Love Inspired® novels and my 2 FREE mystery gifts. After receiving them, if I don't wish to receive any more books, I can return the shipping statement marked "cancel." If I don't cancel, I will receive 4 brand-new novels every month and be billed just $3.99 per book in the U.S., or $4.74 per book in Canada, plus 25¢ shipping and handling per book and applicable taxes, if any*. That's a savings of 20% off the cover price! I understand that accepting the 2 free books and gifts places me under no obligation to buy anything. I can always return a shipment and cancel at any time. Even if I never buy another book from Steeple Hill, the two free books and gifts are mine to keep forever.

113 IDN EF26 313 IDN EF27

Name _____ (PLEASE PRINT)

Address _____ Apt. # _____

City _____ State/Prov. _____ Zip/Postal Code _____

Signature (if under 18, a parent or guardian must sign)

Order online at www.LoveInspiredBooks.com

Or mail to Steeple Hill Reader Service™:
IN U.S.A.: P.O. Box 1867, Buffalo, NY 14240-1867
IN CANADA: P.O. Box 609, Fort Erie, Ontario L2A 5X3

Not valid to current Love Inspired subscribers.

Want to try two free books from another series?
Call 1-800-873-8635 or visit www.morefreebooks.com

* Terms and prices subject to change without notice. NY residents add applicable sales tax. Canadian residents will be charged applicable provincial taxes and GST. This offer is limited to one order per household. All orders subject to approval. Credit or debit balances in a customer's account(s) may be offset by any other outstanding balance owed by or to the customer. Please allow 4 to 6 weeks for delivery.

Your Privacy: Steeple Hill is committed to protecting your privacy. Our Privacy Policy is available online at www.eHarlequin.com or upon request from the Reader Service. From time to time we make our lists of customers available to reputable firms who may have a product or service of interest to you. If you would prefer we not share your name and address, please check here. ☐

LIREG07

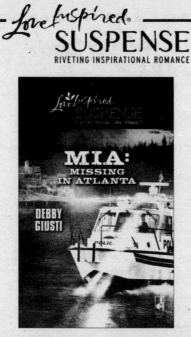

Love Inspired®

TITLES AVAILABLE NEXT MONTH

Don't miss these four stories in March

HEART'S HAVEN by Lois Richer
Pennies from Heaven
Cooking at the Haven, a new outreach mission in Chicago, was chef Cassidy Preston's way to pay back a huge favor. For Tyson St. John, the mission was a place to raise his nephew. Together they could make it their own haven as a family.

A TREASURE WORTH KEEPING by Kathryn Springer
Evie McBride planned a secluded summer running her dad's antique shop. But the teacher in her couldn't ignore a troubled teen who needed tutoring—or the teen's handsome uncle. Would this play-it-safe girl risk her heart for a treasure worth keeping?

MOUNTAIN SANCTUARY by Lenora Worth
Raising her son and running her B and B in rural Arkansas kept Stella Forsythe busy. She wasn't looking for romance until Adam Callahan came to town. The world-weary cop offered his services as a Good Samaritan. With a little prayer, he hoped they could find sanctuary in their budding love.

A SOLDIER'S FAMILY by Cheryl Wyatt
Wings of Refuge
Pararescue jumper Manny Pena had stuck his foot in his mouth when he'd met Celia Munoz. Now he was desperate to make amends. But Celia wasn't having it. Could his growing commitment to her and her troubled son begin to convince her that perhaps she should take her own leap of faith?